Kit didn't have long to wait. The Comanches appeared suddenly and silently from the trees below. Kit pressed back into the cleft and watched first one, then two riders appear between the trees. A moment later a third rider came out of the shadows off to one side. They stopped, studying Kit's tracks, then lifted their eyes to the tall rock before them.

Even though he knew that they could not see him, Kit's skin crawled as their searching eyes scanned the rocky outcropping, probing the deep shadows where he had hidden himself. Kit held his breath, not wanting the steam of it to give away his position. He knew they would circle around behind the rock next. They would rightly guess that this outcropping would be the place for a man on the run to turn and make a stand. They'd be wary of an attack. They'd surely find the fissure where Kit had climbed the crag. And then they would find him.

WESTERN

KIT CARSON

COMANCHE RECKONING

DOUG HAWKINS

LEISURE BOOKS NEW YORK CITY

For Rico, Roxy, and Sarah

A LEISURE BOOK®

November 1998

Published by

Dorchester Publishing Co., Inc.
276 Fifth Avenue
New York, NY 10001

ISBN 0-8439-4453-6

ACKNOWLEDGMENTS

My sincerest thanks to the late Dr. Thomas Edward, who so graciously allowed me to roam freely through his rare and valuable collection of monographs by that nineteenth-century Native American scholar, Professor W. G. F. Smith.

COMANCHE
RECKONING

Chapter One

The stinging blasts bit savagely into Hernando Vigil's bunched fingers as he clutched the sheepskin coat closed against the sharp winter wind. Although well after dark, the faint light from a lopsided moon reflecting off the flying snow and glistening white ground lent an almost eerie feeling of daylight to the forest of low piñon pines through which Hernando was trudging.

With head bent to the wind and his right hand shoved deep into his pocket, wrapped tightly around the pouch of gold coins buried there, Hernando concentrated on putting one foot in front of the other, upon keeping his bearings straight, upon the puffs of gray steam that billowed from his mouth with each labored breath. And although the bitter cold brought violent shivers that wracked his thin body, just holding a vision of Juanita in his thoughts and knowing that tomorrow they would be together again kept a fire blazing within his breast, driving him on, making the cold almost bearable.

Maria Juanita Chacon; the beautiful daughter of that stubborn old *patrón*, Juan de Dios Chacon, could kindle a fire in any man whom she wished. But to Hernando's great good fortune, it was *he* she had chosen!

Or was it such good fortune?

Hernando frowned, thinking back to that morning and what he had done.

What a man would do for the woman he loved! Some would steal for one such as Juanita.

Some might even kill for her.

His fist tightened upon the sack of coins in his pocket. A weight settled upon his shoulders and he softly cursed old Chacon. At once Hernando regretted it and he quickly crossed himself, offering up a hasty prayer to the Blessed Virgin as penance for his sin. Still, he could hardly be blamed for the feelings he held toward Juanita's stern father.

Money!

Was it really all that necessary for happiness where matters of the heart were concerned? And if not, why treat him like a cur just because he happened to be better than most men at not acquiring wealth? Was it his choice he was born of poor parents? Could he help it that he was but a *peón* in the employ of Don Francisco Jaramillo . . . or at least had been up until that morning?

He was but a poor man. It was his lot in life, his cross to bear. It was not his fault. Yet, he wondered, could any other man bring Juanita more happiness than he could?

10

His fist tightened around the pouch again. Well, if money was all that important to her father, he would show Juan de Dios Chacon money!

Another violent shiver grabbed hold of him and shook him like a wolf shakes the life out of a rabbit. It occurred to Hernando suddenly, and for the first time, that he might not make it until tomorrow if he did not come upon some shelter. He had underestimated the fierceness of the storm, the intensity of the cold, and the distance to the crossing of the deep canyon of the Rio Del Norte and then on to La Madera, where Chacon's rancho was headquartered. It had been foolish of him not to have taken a horse before leaving Taos. Hernando had to smile at himself. Horses were one of the few things he truly understood! Women . . . and women whose fathers insisted on wealthy son-in-laws, this was something he had no comprehension of. Why had he overlooked such a simple and obvious matter as taking a horse? After all, what would one more thing matter now to Jaramillo?

He wondered briefly if perhaps he should have stopped at Turley's distillery in Arroyo Hondo when he had passed it earlier that evening. Turley was an amiable fellow who would have given him refuge for the night, a chair by his fire to warm his freezing feet, and a horn of *aguardiente* to warm his insides.

But he hadn't stopped. He had feared that the delay might have given Don Francisco time to catch up with him. He couldn't permit that now.

Ruefully, Hernando looked over his shoulder at the tracks he was leaving in the snow. Well, it could not be helped. Perhaps by morning, if the storm continued, they would be covered over. A horse would have been the smart thing to take, Hernando chided himself again. Then a sudden, wry grin spread across his thin face. Being smart, like being wealthy, was an affliction which had never overly plagued him.

Hernando strove on through the snow and the cold. There was nothing else for him to do now.

Another hour passed. The piñon tree forests gave way to sage-covered flatlands of the high New Mexico desert as the land angled gently toward the great river in the distance. The Rio Del Norte, the Rio Grande as some called it, had its headwaters in the high mountains to the northwest, across the San Luis Valley. Hernando had never been any farther north than the San Luis Valley, but he'd heard a great many stories about those mountains from the friends of Don Francisco, and from the Don's new son-in-law, Charles Bent. Bent had once been a trapper himself, and he still had many close friends among the Rocky Mountain men who traded at Bent's new outpost on the Arkansas River.

Why, just the day before, while Bent and some trappers sat in Don Francisco's home near the fireplace, sipping brandy brought all the way from the United States, he'd heard a fascinating story from one of Bent's close friends, Kit Carson. Kit had been telling them about the big river called the Missouri, and of the grand boats which use steam power to climb the wide waters, thousands of miles from the nearest settlements. Kit Carson had been telling Charles Bent all about the trading forts at the Missouri's headwaters, for this was something which Bent was greatly concerned

12

about, having just established his own trading house a couple of years earlier.

Hernando had listened to their talk from a back room where he had been oiling Don Francisco's saddle while Geraldine, the Jaramillos' house helper, was polishing the family's silverware in preparation for the upcoming Christmas dinner. He could hardly believe what he had heard. A river that was more than half a mile wide! Why, even the impressive Rio Del Norte was only a few hundred feet wide at its broadest.

Hernando shivered again and the memory faded, pushed aside by the bitter cold cutting through his cotton britches, and working its way though the sheepskin coat. How much more of this could he take? It had been foolish to start out on a day like this. Perhaps he should have waited. But he had so wanted to spend Christmas day with his love. He had told Juanita of his plans to come to her the week before when she and her mother had come to Taos to shop. She would be waiting for him, he knew, and he could not have waited . . .

Something caught his eye. He stopped and ducked behind a clump of sage. Ahead, in a stand of cottonwood trees nestled down inside a protected arroyo, came the red and yellow flicker of a fire. Around the fire he spied some men, three, he thought, or was it four? He was not sure. At the mouth of the arroyo, where the naked cottonwoods were bunched together, Hernando counted four horses.

His first thought was to swing wide of these men and continue on his way, but then an idea came to him. A horse was all that he lacked to assure a successful journey to La Madera. A horse would make traveling so much easier, and for anyone who might be following him, that much more difficult. A plan slowly took shape, and using what cover he could find, Hernando worked his way toward the animals.

As Hernando drew nearer to the horses, he saw that the animals were still saddled. So, he thought, these men were not planning to stay long in this place. So much the better. Saddled, the animals were ready to ride. But it also meant that he had to work fast.

Seth Wilson shifted his position by the fire and gave a soft groan.

"The shoulder, it is hurting you again?" Tomas Beaubien asked, looking over.

"Again?" Wilson gruffed. "When has it ever stopped hurting?" Wilson was a husky man, not overly tall, with a thick, bull neck and powerful shoulders, hidden now beneath a heavy bearskin coat.

"*Sí*, but it seems to hurt more when the weather, she turns cold, like tonight, heh?"

"Yeah, it hurts more. What can you expect with a hunk of lead buried under the shoulder blade? Damn his mangy hide!"

"Who are you damning tonight, *señor*?" the third man, Pedro Trujillo, inquired.

Wilson shot the Mexican a narrow glance. "Who do you think?"

Pedro chuckled.

Tomas said, "You need not ask such a foolish question, my cousin. Who has *Señor* Wilson ever cursed since we have known him—how long is it now? Two years already?"

Wilson pulled a burning brand from the fire, ignoring the chuckles of his two companions and the sudden spike of pain in his left shoulder. He put the flame to the bowl of his pipe, and when he had his tobacco burning he said, "You think it's real funny, don't you? Maybe someday I'll put a bullet in your back, Pedro, and see how you like it."

"You are a lucky man just to be alive, heh?" Tomas observed.

"Yeah," Wilson groused. "Such luck I have." He was in a foul mood tonight. He'd left a warm bed and a willing woman back in Santa Fe that morning, had ridden all day through one of the worst winter storms New Mexico had seen in years. And now he was squatting in this arroyo trying to keep warm over their small fire . . . in the company of two Mexicans whom he only half liked on good days—and today wasn't one of them. Wilson's shoulder never completely stopped hurting, but on cold days like this, the ache deep down beneath the blade was pure misery and Wilson remembered—remembered the man who had put the bullet there.

Damn his worthless soul! Wilson went to bed at night cursing the man who had shot him in the back as he was fleeing. He woke up in the morning with the same curse on his lips. And throughout the day he reviled the man, vowing that some day he'd have his revenge. Someday he would meet up with Kit Carson again and when he did . . .

"Why do you not have a doctor cut the bullet out of your back?" Tomas asked.

"Nobody takes a knife to my hide, Beaubien," Wilson barked impatiently. "I'll live with it." He stared down the dark length of the arroyo. "Where the hell is your brother anyway?"

Tomas shrugged, unconcerned. "He will be here. You know how it is to make the deal with the Indians." Tomas inclined his head at the flimsy tent flapping in the wind nearby. But we have what the Comanches want, and they have what we want. In the end, Diego and Broken Nose will see eye-to-eye, and then Diego will lead them here."

Seth Wilson had come south a couple of years earlier, hoping to evade the authorities who might be hunting him from the States. He had heard that the beaver was plentiful in the rivers of Northern Mexico, but what he had found instead were streams nearly trapped out and an alcalde sitting in the Palace of the Governors in Santa Fe who was reluctant to issue trapping permits to any American.

Wilson had been in Santa Fe, in a dusty cantina, lamenting his bad luck over a pint of *aguardiente* when he had happened to meet Diego Beaubien. Diego, his brother Tomas, and their cousin Pedro were quietly trading guns to the Comanches in exchange for some of the finest mustangs money could buy. Making a good living at it, too. They had recently lost a partner over some disagreement. Wilson had never asked for the details, and none were ever given. They were looking for a fourth man to take his place and Wilson liked the sound of gold in the shape of good horseflesh, so he joined up with these *Comancheros*.

No matter how far a man rode these days, it seemed he could never escape government regulations. Just as it had been to trap Mexican beaver, so it was with Mexican commerce; the alcalde's blessings were required to trade with the Comanches. But the way Diego saw it, the less the Mexican government knew about his business the better he liked it. So, without the necessary permits, and the taxes that would have followed, Diego's little clandestine business thrived. But trading without a license also meant meeting the Comanches far from the prying eyes of the alcalde and his minions. And that translated into late-night meetings like this one.

"He could have at least picked a better day to make his deals," Wilson complained.

"Diego knows what he is doing."

Just then one of their horses nickered softly. Something about the sound caught the ears of these men who made their living with horses, and riveted their attention. Tomas gave Pedro a quick glance. "Go see about that," he said in Spanish.

Without having to be told, Pedro backtracked up the arroyo, away from where the horses were picketed, then climbed the frozen slope to its rim. In the soft glow of moonlight against the falling snow, Wilson watched Pedro's shadowy form creep forward toward the horses until the dark trees at the arroyo's mouth swallowed him up.

"Indians?" Wilson whispered, taking up his buffalo rifle and slipping off the leather covering from around its lock.

"Perhaps," Tomas said, his breath hanging in the icy air as he reached inside his heavy coat for a pistol.

Just then all the horses began to whinny. There followed almost at once the sharp snap of a

17

branch and the sound of a struggle. Instantly Wilson and Tomas sprang to their feet and dashed for the place where their animals had been tied. Wilson caught sight of the two struggling men. Jogging to his right into the stand of trees, he grabbed hold of the collar of a sheepskin coat, dragged the stranger off of Pedro, and pressed the barrel of his rifle into the man's chest.

Tomas arrived a second later. "Are you all right, *amigo*?"

Pedro picked himself up and brushed the snow from his clothes. "*Sí*, I caught this *hombre* trying to steal one of our horses."

They looked down at the man beneath the muzzle of Wilson's rifle. "Who are you?" Tomas demanded.

"Do not shoot me!" the man pleaded, covering his head with his arms.

"Why not? You were trying to steal our horses. What is your name?"

"Hernando. Hernando Vigil. I was not going to steal the horse."

Tomas threw up his hands. "Hah! What were you doing then?" he said, mocking. "Making love to her?"

"No."

"I ask one more time. What were you doing?"

Hernando stammered and glanced helplessly up at them. Wilson could see that he was stalling, trying to think of a story. He drew back the hammer of his rifle.

"I was only trying to get warm," Hernando blurted lamely. "The night is very cold."

"Then why didn't you just come to our fire?" Wilson demanded.

"I . . . I was afraid. I thought perhaps you might be . . . might be Indians."

"Indians?" Tomas stared at the horses and their heavy Mexican saddles. "Indians don't use saddles like these," he pointed out.

Hernando shifted his view between Tomas and the muzzle of Wilson's rifle. "I know that now, *Señor*. I am not very smart. I am only a *peón*."

"Who is your *patrón*?"

"Don Francisco Jaramillo."

"Jaramillo? I do not know him."

Pedro said, "This man is lying, Tomas. He was trying to untie the reins when I came up on him."

"Should I kill him?" Wilson growled.

"Yes. I think perhaps you should."

"No, wait, please. I was not going to steal the animal. I was only looking him over. I . . . I was going to offer to buy him from you. It is the truth."

Tomas laughed. "Buy him? What money does a *peón* have to buy a horse with? Especially one of this breeding, heh?"

"I have money. I have gold!" Hernando blurted.

Wilson's eyes narrowed. "Gold?"

"*Sí.* I will buy the animal from you."

Tomas reached out and moved Wilson's rifle barrel from Hernando's chest. He hunkered down beside the frightened man. "Gold? You have this gold with you, now?"

"I do," Hernando answered nervously.

"Let me see it."

Hernando hesitated.

Tomas glanced at Wilson. "Shoot him."

"No! I will show it to you." Hernando dug at his coat pocket and came out with a pouch. Tomas

19

snatched it away, worked the thong loose, and poured the coins into his palm.

"Sweet Mary," Pedro exclaimed. "He does have gold."

Hernando sat up, eyes wide with fear. "You can keep it. Just let me go."

"Without the horse?" The mocking tone had returned to Tomas's voice.

"*Sí.* Just permit me to leave. It is all I ask."

Tomas thought it over a moment. "No. I think not. You would not have bought the horse. You would have taken it. You are a horse thief, and I am in my right to have you killed." He glanced up at Wilson and nodded his head.

Wilson swung the rifle toward Hernando.

Throwing his hands in front of his face, Hernando cried, "If you kill me now, what will ever happen to the second pouch of gold?"

Tomas stopped Wilson as his finger was curling inside the trigger guard. "There is another pouch?"

Still hiding his eyes, Hernando nodded his head. "I buried it, after I left Taos."

"Hmm?" Tomas looked at his two partners. "Bring him back to the fire. We will wait for Diego's return. He will know what to do."

Chapter Two

"I'll wager the weasel just said that to save his scrawny neck." Wilson winced as he reached for a pot of coffee sitting in a bank of coals. Pouring himself another cup, he said, "Where the hell is your brother anyway, Tomas? It must be nearly midnight."

"You are in a hurry to be somewhere else, *Señor* Wilson?"

Wilson glared at the Mexican. "I got me a woman and a bottle of American whiskey waiting back in Santa Fe, and I've got a powerful hankering to spend time with both of 'em. Hell, tomorrow is Christmas Eve. I can think of a lot of ways I'd rather be spending it than sitting out here freezing my tail off and looking at your ugly face."

"Perhaps."

Wilson glanced over.

Tomas grinned. "I mean, perhaps the weasel

was lying." He tossed the pouch of gold coins into the air and caught it, shoving it back into his pocket.

"What are you intending to do with all that gold?" Wilson asked suspiciously.

"Wait until Diego returns. He will know what to do with it."

Wilson snorted. "How long are you going to let your big brother do your thinking for you?"

"Tomas!" Pedro barked, urgency edging his voice.

"What is it?" he answered, his dark eyes still confronting Wilson's.

"We have a visitor!" came Pedro's harsh whisper.

From out of the darkness a man on horseback rode up the arroyo. Dressed in a long, shaggy buffaloskin coat that hung down to his stirrups, the stranger came through the blowing snow. A wolfskin hat covered most of his head; only eyes, nose, and mouth were visible. He carried a long rifle in one hand and held the reins in the other. He rode straight for the fire, coming to a halt in front of them.

For a long moment, no one spoke.

"Señor, welcome to our humble fire," Tomas said finally, recovering from the surprise of the man's sudden appearance.

Wilson's hand crept back for the rifle at his side.

The stranger silently sat there a moment longer, his searching eyes taking in every detail of their camp. They flicked briefly to the flapping tent, then settled on Wilson, narrowing slightly as if trying to recall something. Finally the man spoke.

"Where is he?"

Something in the voice made Wilson's skin crawl. Something he could not identify. A voice from out of his past, and he knew that this was no social call.

Tomas gave a short laugh. "*Señor*, there is no one else here. See, it is just the three of us. We have coffee. *Muy caliente*, good for a night such as this." He reached for the pot with his left hand, leaving his right near the buttons of his heavy coat.

Pedro eased back a little, just outside the glow of the low fire, and buried a hand inside the deep pocket of his wool coat.

The stranger relaxed some and said, "Whal, that's right neighborly of you."

Tomas grinned. "Come and join us. Here, I will pour you some." Knocking the grinds out of his own tin cup, he refilled it with fresh coffee.

"It's a cold night to be out," the stranger said evenly. It was a simple statement, but the question behind it did not escape them.

Tomas turned it back on him. "Such a cold night to be riding alone, no?"

"What makes you think I'm alone?"

Tomas glanced down the arroyo. "I see no one else here, *Señor*."

Wilson had been puzzling over the voice. "Do I know you, stranger?"

The man looked back at him, his eyes narrowing again. "Maybe, maybe not. It's a big country and I move around a lot." It was plain he had been pondering the same question too.

"What's your name?"

"First tell me where he is. Then we'll talk."

"He? . . . He?" Tomas said, exasperated. "Who is

23

this he? I tell you, there is only the three of us."

"That's a lie."

Tomas's view turned icy, like the wind that rippled the fur of his collar. "No man calls me a liar, *Señor*."

"I say it as I see it, mister. I've trailed him to this spot and I know he's here, in that tent over thar maybe. I want him. Bring him out."

Wilson's eyes suddenly came together. "I do know you!" He grabbed for the rifle.

"Don't!" the stranger barked, but even as he spoke Tomas was drawing a pistol from under his coat, and Pedro had pulled a short pistol free of his pocket.

The stranger swung his buffalo rifle and pulled the trigger. Flame stabbed out into the darkness as the boom echoed between the arroyo's steep walls. The bullet took Tomas in the chest, picked him up and slammed him back into the snow.

Wilson brought his rifle around.

Striving to keep his seat upon the startled horse, the stranger flung his rifle aside and both hands plunged under the thick, shaggy coat. A brace of pistols leaped free of it, booming together. A bullet struck Wilson, kicking him back and to the left even as the second bullet snapped Pedro's head back, nearly flipping him beyond the firelight to the right.

Slowly the echo faded away from the arroyo. Beyond the stranger's smoking pistols lay three dead men. Tucking them back under his coat, he swung off the horse, speaking in low, soothing tones to calm the nervous animal. He picked up his rifle, brushed the snow from its lock, and blew on it to clear the nipple.

Grimacing, he checked the three men. When he came to Wilson, he paused and his forehead furrowed as he studied the face behind the dark beard. Straightening, his view swept the campsite and settled upon the flapping tent.

Drawing a tomahawk from under the coat, the stranger moved toward it. He stopped just outside, listening, then in a flurry of motion he yanked back the door flap and lunged inside. At his feet lay Hernando Vigil, hands and feet bound tight, a rag stuffed in his mouth. Hernando's wide eyes stared up at him. Alongside the Mexican were two long crates.

A faint smile touched the stranger's lips, lifting the grim set of his mouth.

"Hernando," he said softly, shaking his head. He dug the wad of cloth from the Mexican's mouth.

Hernando took a huge breath, as if he had not been able to breathe until just then, and with a great sigh of relief he nearly sobbed, "*Señor* Carson! Thank God it is you!"

The frown returned to Kit's face. "It might be a bit early to be thanking Deity, Hernando," he said flatly.

"Please, untie me. They made the knots too tight. My hands are almost frozen and soon my fingers, they will fall off."

"Not so fast, Hernando." Kit pushed the tomahawk back under his belt and hunkered down, setting his rifle onto the frozen ground. He searched the helpless man, turned Hernando's pockets inside out and came up empty-handed—except for a fistful of jerked beef. "All right, what have you done with it."

"It?" Hernando gave him a blank look and a fal-

25

tering laugh. "Surely, *Señor* Carson, you play a game with me. Please, untie my hands."

"You know, Hernando, I ain't never seen a man's fingers freeze solid. Reckon they'd just snap off like a frozen twist of tobacco when they did."

"*Señor* Carson, you have had your little joke. My hands, please."

"Joke?" Kit pulled thoughtfully at his chin.

"*Sí*, it is a little joke, is it not?"

Kit stood. "I'll be back in the morning to see how them fingers are coming along," and as he turned away he mumbled to himself, "bet they'll snap like a twig."

"Wait!"

Kit glanced back from the door flap.

Hernando laughed. "I didn't know what you meant at first, *Señor* Carson. Now I think I understand. It is, perhaps, that little pouch of gold coins you speak of?"

"Don Francisco doesn't think eight hundred dollars is so little."

He shrugged and grinned easily, but his dark eyes shifted back and forth nervously, as if scurrying to catch a fleeting thought. "To a man of the *patrón*'s wealth, it may be important, yes, but to a poor man like me, it is a great treasure. Especially when you know the reason I had to take the money."

"Had to take it?"

"*Sí*, I had to take it."

"Thar ain't any reason I can think of for a man to steal, except maybe as a matter of life or death."

"But that's exactly what it is, *Señor* Carson. Life or death! For what is life without my beautiful Juanita Chacon, except a slow death, as sure a death as if you shot me right here where I lay."

Kit scoffed. "You're talking like you got feathers for brains, Hernando. You trying to tell me you stole the gold because of a woman?"

He nodded his head.

"Now I know you got feathers for brains. Tell me where it is."

"All right, I will tell you, but you will not like it."

"Where is it?" Kit was at the end of his patience.

"First my hands."

"I'll be back in the morning."

"I hid the gold," he said when Kit turned back out the door. "Five or six miles back."

"Whal, then I reckon we better go and unhide it, Hernando." Kit drew his butcher knife and sawed the leather thongs binding Hernando's wrists and ankles.

The skinny Mexican sat up, rubbing the circulation back into his wrists.

"Kit! Kit, you here?" came a voice from outside.

"I'm inside the tent, Charlie. I found the thief."

"Good God, what happened here?"

Kit swept aside the door and stepped out into the swirling snow. Charles Bent was standing among the bodies, his rifle gripped tightly in his fists.

Bent was ten years older than Kit. He had gray, intelligent eyes, a broad forehead, and hair so dark that some people mistook him for a French Canadian, or even a half-breed Indian. He spoke French fluently, and so many dialects of Indian that it was not difficult to see how the error might come about. But his ancestry was English, his forebears having fled to America in 1638. Charles, like his friend Kit, stood only five feet seven inches tall, and like Kit, he had spent most of his youth in Missouri, then traveled westward following the beaver trail. But unlike Kit, Charles Bent had a keen business mind and was already well on the road to great wealth, a road presently being made smooth and sure by the recent completion of his trading house on the Arkansas River near the mouth of the Purgatory River. And by his marriage only one week earlier to Don Francisco Jaramillo's widowed daughter, Maria Ignacia.

Kit and Charlie had been following Hernando's tracks when they crossed a second set. Kit had followed one while Bent had scouted the other.

"I came as soon as I heard the shooting," Bent said. "Would have ended up here anyway. These are the men who made that second set. What happened?"

"They didn't want to turn Hernando over and went for thar guns instead."

"Wonder who they are."

"Don't know. But thar's two crates of rifles inside that tent. They seemed to be waiting for someone. Offhand, I'd say they was up to no good."

Bent glanced up. *"Comancheros?"*

"That would be my guess."

Hernando appeared under the door flap and stopped beside Kit, staring at the bodies.

Bent reached down and turned Pedro's face around. Kit's bullet had gone through the forehead, taking a dollar-size chuck of skull out the back of the man's head. "Don't know him." Bent moved to Tomas. "Don't know this one either." He knelt in the snow next to the third body. "This one is American." Bent narrowed his eyes and frowned, putting a hand near the man's mouth. "And he's still alive."

Kit peered closely at the man's face for the first time. "Wilson!"

"You know him?"

"I know him all right," Kit said tightly, not trying to hide the bitterness in his voice. "Remember me telling you about them fellows who kidnapped a gal from her home in Independence, and how they dragged her clear out to the Rocky Mountains?"

"I remember. Wasn't that the time you met that Indian you ride with sometimes?"

"Gray Feather? That's right." Kit looked down at Wilson. "Whal, this is the one I shot while he was making a break for his horse. He managed to get away." Kit frowned. "Looks like I shot him again, and I still didn't kill the polecat."

They opened Wilson's coat and found that the bullet had gone low and to the right, smashing a rib.

Kit shook his head. "A little more to the left is all she needed to be. Whal, that's what I get for trying it left-handed."

"Don't kick yourself too hard, Kit. You did your best considering the odds you were up against. What do you want to do with him?"

Kit grimaced. Wilson was a rattlesnake that should have had his head hacked off years ago. He and his partners had terrorized a young woman named Marjory Holmes for months, brutally raping her and keeping her hidden away in their mountain cabin. Kit had saved the girl, killed one of the men involved, and sent another back to the States with Marjory's father to answer for his crimes. But Wilson had managed to escape.

What Kit *wanted* to do was skin the varmint alive and hang him up for crowbait. But what he knew he *had* to do was something else entirely.

"Reckon we ought to bring him back with us. I know a man in Missouri who'll be right pleased to get his hands on the critter."

Wilson came around. His eyes opened and narrowed at Kit's face. Through teeth clenched in pain he said, "I knew it was you, Carson. You done shot me again, you sunuvabitch."

"Looks like I did at that. But I didn't shoot you good enough."

"You'll wish you had."

Bent let out a soft whistle and said, "This one is full of vinegar, isn't he, Kit?"

"Put him atop a horse and see how long it takes to bounce some sweetness into him." Kit glanced around for Hernando and discovered the Mexican rummaging through the pockets of one of the dead men. "What are you doing?"

Hernando slipped a hand into his own pocket, and grinned sheepishly. "I was only trying to discover who they were, *Señor* Carson. Maybe they have family, no?"

"If they do, I'm sure Wilson here can tell us all about them. Go over yonder and bring those animals here."

"*Sí*, right away." Hernando trotted down the arroyo.

Bent strode to the tent and stepped past the door flap. He stuck his head out a moment later. "Seems a shame to leave these rifles behind."

Kit knew that Charlie was thinking like a businessman now. He couldn't stand to see marketable merchandise go to waste. If the owners never came to claim them, he could sell them at 100 percent profit at his trading house. "Take them with us. I saw a pack animal with the others. If they're stolen, maybe we can find the owner. If not, well, these boys aren't gonna need them anymore and we don't want to let them lay around for the Comanches to find."

Hernando returned with the animals. Kit and Charlie tied the crates of rifles to the pack frames, and boosted Seth Wilson up onto a horse.

Turning to the Mexican, Kit gave Hernando a withering stare. "All right, suppose you show me where you hid Don Francisco Jaramillo's gold. Then we'll go pay Mr. Jaramillo a visit. He's anxious to see you."

"Right anxious," Bent added ominously.

Hernando choked down a lump in his throat and managed a weak grin.

They saddled up and moved out, leaving the bodies lying in the snow by the crackling fire. The wolves and coyotes would make short work of them.

Icy wind swirled snow into the arroyo, ruffling the hair of the dead men, drawing the last bit of heat from their bodies. The fire died down to a pile of glowing embers. In a short time, even the coals buried deep beneath the ashes would be cold to the touch. . . .

Long Runner held his hand upon the embers, not feeling any heat in them. He carefully scanned the deserted campsite. Assuring himself that there was no danger here, he shifted his view back to the two bodies sprawled before him and waved an arm. A dozen riders emerged from the shadows. In a moment the arroyo was filled with Comanches and a herd of horses, kept bunched together by four skilled herdsmen. Steam puffed from the animals' nostrils, as it did from the riders, who all wore heavy buffalo robes.

Among the Indians rode one Mexican. Diego Beaubien came closer and his view shot to the bodies on the ground. Instantly he leaped from the saddle and went to one of them.

"Tomas!" he cried, taking the lifeless body into his arms. He held the man for a long moment and tears stung his eyes. Laying him gently back into the snow, Diego's hand came up with cold, sticky blood clinging thickly to his fingers. Shocked, he glanced at one of the Comanches still astride his pony. "They have been murdered."

"He was your brother?"

Diego nodded his head.

Broken Nose, the war chief, barked an order. Immediately three warriors slid off the back of their ponies and fanned out, searching the night for signs. The chief's attention came back to Diego.

"This is not a good night for you," he said in Spanish.

"No, it is not." Diego stood, his eyes still fixed on the body at his feet.

Broken Nose said, "The rifles?"

Still in shock, Diego wiped his hand on the snow and nodded his head toward the tent.

Broken Nose sent men to retrieve them.

The two dogs traveling with the party trotted over and sniffed the bodies.

"Get away from them!" Diego roared, kicking at the animals.

More wolf than dog, they crouched and growled, baring long curving fangs at him.

Broken Nose spoke a sharp command in the Comanche tongue and reluctantly the dogs backed down. They trotted away from the bodies and sat on either side of the war chief's horse. Broken Nose reached down and petted the head of one of the dogs affectionately.

"The rifles are not here," an Indian called from the door flap of the tent.

His words shook Diego from his stupor. "Not there?" He strode across the arroyo and checked the tent for himself. Finding the two crates missing, Diego said to Broken Nose, "Whoever killed Tomas and Pedro must have taken the rifles too."

At that moment one of the scouts shouted from the rim of the arroyo that they had discovered tracks leading away.

"I will find the murderers!" Diego vowed. "And the rifles too, Broken Nose."

The Comanche nodded his head. "You find rifles and we will trade. No rifles and we take horses back with us."

"I'll find them!" Diego declared again. With help from the Indians, Diego put Tomas and Pedro across their horses and tied them in place.

"There is still one man missing," Diego told Broken Nose. "The gringo, Wilson. They must have taken him with them."

Broken Nose pointed to an impression in the snow, nearly covered over by the blizzard. "He has been wounded, I think. They cannot travel quickly with a wounded man."

Mounting up, the band moved out, following the tracks with Broken Nose's two dogs trotting in the lead.

Chapter Three

Huddled deep within his coat, Kit Carson led the
party back toward the piñon forests and Taos,
which by his reckoning was yet twenty miles
ahead. He was amazed that Hernando had been
able to make such good distance on foot, but then
the Mexican had left very early that morning—
sometime before daylight. Don Francisco had discovered the gold coins missing after breakfast, and
if it had not been for the tell-tale tracks leading
away from the house, which Kit had instantly identified as belonging to Don Francisco Jaramillo's
groom, Hernando, the identity of the thief might
not have been known until Hernando's sudden dis-
appearance pointed the incriminating finger.

Hernando's trail had not been difficult to follow.
It was impossible to hide one's footsteps in fresh
snow, and it was only much later in the day that
the snowfall had become heavy enough to possi-

bly cover them over. Then tracking would have been much more difficult, if not impossible. Kit and Don Francisco's new son-in-law had started out at once, but by then Hernando's lead was already hours old.

Don Francisco had been stunned by the theft. Hernando had been a trusted employee of the Jaramillo household for years. Kit had spoken to Hernando a couple of times at the Jaramillo house, and he'd met him once years earlier when the Mexican had worked for a horse breeder named Saavadra. Taos was not that large a town, and everyone knew everyone else.

It was fortunate for Jaramillo that Christmas was just two days away, and that the wedding of his daughter, Ignacia, had taken place only a week earlier. The house was still full of guests, including Kit Carson, who had come out of the mountains to attend the occasion. Of all the men there, Kit was the most experienced tracker. And it was only he and Charles Bent who had set out that morning to find the thief, for trailing Hernando was not considered either a very challenging task, or a very dangerous one.

Seth Wilson groaned. Kit glanced back. The man was having trouble staying in the saddle. He clutched the horn in both hands and leaned forward almost upon the horse's neck.

Returning his view to the timbered trail ahead, Kit longed for the warm comfort of Jaramillo's large adobe house, with its many big fireplaces. It was already too late to get back to Taos tonight, but at least they would be back by morning. Christmas Eve was a time to spend with friends; it was not time to be on the trail, in a blizzard, in the company of two scoundrels. Don Francisco was planning a Christmas Eve fandango, and Kit did love to kick up his heels with the pretty *señoritas*. But more than that, December 24 was Kit's birthday, although it hardly ever got remembered, falling right on the toes of Christmas as it did.

Kit turned at a sudden commotion behind him. Hernando had kicked his horse into motion and had expertly maneuvered alongside Wilson's animal. He shot out a hand just in time to stop Wilson from slipping from the saddle. They reined to a halt, and Bent rode up on the other side of the man, steadying him.

"He isn't going to make it this way, Kit," Bent said. Seth Wilson had fainted.

"Leave him behind," Hernando suggested. "He's a *muy malo hombre*."

"I'm half-inclined to agree with Hernando. Tie him over his saddle."

Bent grinned at his friend. "You really don't like that fellow very much, do you, Kit? I thought you wanted to get him back to the States alive."

Giving a tight frown, Kit reluctantly nodded his head. Bent was right. Kit could find no pity in his heart for Seth Wilson. Every time he looked at Wilson's face he remembered the terribly frightened eyes of the girl they had brutalized for so many months. But Kit was practical enough not to let his feelings rule over what he knew he had to do. "You're right, Charlie. Reckon we need to build us a travois."

"There are some aspens down that draw," Bent noted, pointing toward a nearby ravine where the ice of a frozen stream glistened in the moonlight.

Doug Hawkins

The men swung off their saddles and laid Wilson out on the snow. Kit gathered some dry kindling from under a fallen log and, striking sparks from his tinder kit, got a small fire started. They moved Wilson near it, and warmed their hands before getting to work. Down in the ravine Kit and Bent felled two young aspen trees. Using rope and thin branches, they constructed a crude litter which they intended to fasten to Wilson's horse.

While Kit and Bent were occupied with the travois, Hernando saw his opportunity to slip away into the night unnoticed. But he had to be sly about it. Biding his time, he waited until no one was looking. Quickly he stepped behind a nearby piñon tree. His heart pounded his ribs as he waited to see if his absence would be discovered. When an alarm wasn't immediately sounded, Hernando briefly weighed the possibilities of taking one of the horses and fleeing . . . but no, that would never work. Kit Carson had already trailed him once. Hernando knew that he could never elude Kit so long as he left even one horse behind.

But perhaps . . . ?

The animals were tied to the branches of a pine tree. Blowing steam into his hands to warm them, Hernando carefully rounded the back of the tree, gritting his teeth at the crunch of snow beneath his boots, which sounded horribly loud to him just then. He came to the place where the reins had been tied into its branches and paused to listen to the two men talking below. So far no one had noticed him missing. Working quickly, Hernando untied the animals and quietly led them away.

After a few dozen feet, Hernando began to whisper soft, soothing sounds to the horses. They had become skittish and Hernando could not chance a nervous whinny that might give him away. He had a natural ability where horses were concerned, and his hopes climbed as a minute passed, and then two. With a horse, he could easily make La Madera by morning. He would then openly profess his love for Juan de Dios Chacon's daughter, and ask for her hand in marriage. If money was such an important issue to the old man, then money Hernando would show him!

A vision of Maria Juanita Chacon filled his brain, temporarily shoving everything else to the side. For a brief moment the warm glow of her beauty melted the winter snow that blanketed everything in white. Then the urgency of what he was doing returned to him. The vision faded and the wind bit through his heavy coat, reminding him that he was not yet free of Kit Carson and Charlie Bent, and that the time for daydreaming was still far off. But just the same, Hernando's spirits were practically soaring.

He led the animals around an outcropping of rock which cut off the firelight flickering though the trees. Hernando singled out his horse and shoved a foot into the stirrup. Something icy cold settled hard against his neck, and he froze at its touch.

Kit's voice reached ominously out to him from the night. "Where do you think you're going, Hernando?"

Slowly Hernando looked around and found himself staring into the huge bore of Kit's 32-gauge buffalo rifle. He managed a quick, high-pitched laugh in spite of himself. "*Señor* Carson, it is you. I am relieved. I thought at first it might be Indians."

"Uh-huh. Looks to me like you was trying to light out on us, Hernando."

"Light out? Oh, no, I would never do that."

"Then what do you call this?"

Hernando glanced at the horses. An expression of shock at the immensity of the apparent misunderstanding came to his face. "This? Why, I was only taking the horses to find some grass for them. See, look." He kicked at the snow piled against the outcropping, exposing the stiff, brown grass that had grown there the summer before. Quickly yanking a handful of it out, Hernando fed it to one of the horses. "See, *Señor* Carson, they are hungry, no?"

Kit's frown deepened.

Hernando looked most downhearted at Kit's accusation. "I only wanted to be of some help while you and *Señor* Bent were making ready the litter."

"Mmm."

Charles Bent came around the other side of the rock. "So, you found the weasel," he said, obviously relieved not to be left afoot so far from home. He wiped the snow from the pistol he was holding and opened his coat, tucking the weapon into an inside pocket.

Hernando pouted.

"Reckon we need to tie you up from here on out?"

"Oh, no, *Señor* Carson, you do not need to do that. I should have told you before I took the horses, no?"

Kit shook his head. "Hernando, I don't reckon I have ever met such a lying fool before."

He shrugged his shoulders. "If it is so, then it is because of love."

"What is this balderdash about love?" Bent scoffed.

Hernando looked at him. "You of all men should ask such a question? You who only last Sunday stood in the church before the padre and took the *patrón's* daughter to be your wife?"

Kit said, "Hernando stole Don Francisco's gold to impress the father of some filly he's got his eye on."

"Is that so? Anyone I know?"

Hernando started to speak her name, then he stopped and merely shook his head. "I do not think you would know her, *Señor* Bent."

They escorted Hernando and the horses back to the fire and fed more wood into it, warming their hands over the flames for a few minutes. Afterwards, they hauled the crude travois to Wilson's horse and tied it to the saddle.

"Reckon that will do in a pinch," Kit observed, standing back to inspect their handiwork. "I've seen prettier ones, but it's stout enough to get us back to Taos."

Bent was hunkered down near the fire, soaking in its heat. "That's as far as it needs to go."

Kit hunched down near the flame too, peering at his friend. He rubbed his palms together, held them out to the heat, and said, "We can stay the night here, or push on." He glanced at the clouds and the moon, which was peeking through a break in them. It had crept lower in the sky since they rescued Hernando from the *Comancheros*. "Pulling that travois will slow us down some, Charlie. Waiting for daylight will make the going easier."

41

"I've thought about it, Kit. But to tell you the truth, I'm anxious to be done with this job. I'd just as soon push on. Besides, staying the night won't do Wilson any good. He needs someplace warm and dry, and to be seen by a doctor."

Kit glanced at Wilson. The outlaw was moaning softly where he lay upon the snow. Oddly, the lump of ice that had formed in Kit's heart toward the wounded man had not thawed in the least. The way he felt right then, he could walk away and leave Wilson to the wolves, and never look back . . . and that unnerved Kit just a mite. There was such a thing as compassion. But somehow, it didn't seem to apply here. But Bent was right. They needed to get back to Taos as soon as possible.

"We'll keep moving."

Bent helped Kit carry Wilson to the travois and lay him upon it.

Wilson's eyes opened. "Water," he asked, licking his dry lips.

Bent fetched a tin cup from his saddlebags and melted some snow in it for Wilson. The drink seemed to revive the wounded man some.

"Where are we?" Wilson croaked when Bent took the cup from his lips.

"About twenty miles north of Taos." Bent reached inside his coat for a cheroot. As he did so the butt of his pistol peeked out.

Wilson's eyes shifted and narrowed.

Bent caught the look and grinned. "You want one of these?" he asked, waving the short cigar in front of him.

Wilson glanced at the cigar. "Yeah. Sure."

Bent took a second one from an inside pocket,

lit them both at the fire, and gave one to Wilson. When he looked over, Kit was frowning. Bent chuckled "Don't tell me you want one too?"

"Don't coddle him, Charlie. He ain't worth it."

Bent laughed. "I've never seen you like this, Kit."

"You don't try to make a rabid dog comfortable, Charlie. You just shoot him."

Bent grinned and went back to the fire, kicked snow over it. The snow sizzled and steamed against the hot rocks. "Well, then let's get this rabid dog on to Taos, where we can turn him over to the alcalde."

"I'm not giving him over to the alcalde."

"Oh?"

"As far as I know he hasn't broken any Mexican laws. The alcalde won't hold him. He's going back to Missouri soon as he's fit enough to travel. I'll take him myself if I have to. I want him to stand for his crimes in the States." Kit turned to Hernando. "Do I have to tie you to that thar saddle, or will you behave yourself?"

"*Señor* Carson," he said innocently. "You can trust me. I will not try to escape again."

"Escape? I thought you were only taking our horses to grass?"

Hernando gave Kit a crooked grin. "But I was, *Señor*," he replied.

Kit shook his head. "If only you could lie half as good as you sit a horse, Hernando. How far is it to the place where you hid the gold?"

"It is ahead. I will show you. I only hope I can find it again," Hernando added, as if speaking to himself.

They mounted up and started along the trail again. It was slower going now, burdened by the

travois, leaving two deep furrows in the snow behind them. It would be well past daylight by time
they arrived back at Taos. Kit thought of the coffee Don Francisco would give them upon their ar-
rival, and of the hearty breakfast Francisco's wife
and daughters would prepare. He tried not to ponder unpleasant thoughts, but somehow Seth Wilson kept creeping back into his mind.

If his bullet had only gone three inches more to
the left the problem of Seth Wilson would be far
behind him now, dead in the snow like his two
partners.

Worry creases deepened in Kit's face as he
thought about the incident. The more he turned
it over in his mind, the more the question of what
those men were doing out there weighed down
upon him. They seemed to have been waiting for
someone.

But for who?

The Comanches?

But there was nothing illegal in trading with the
Comanches. So why was the camp so far away
from any of the main trade routes? Unless these
Comancheros were working without the proper
permits from the alcalde.

That would explain the lonely campsite, and
that would also explain the rifles.

Suddenly the hair at the nape of Kit's neck stiffened as the truth dawned on him. They *had* been
waiting for the Comanches!

And that meant . . .

Kit glanced over his shoulder at the deep furrows being cut into the ground by the travois.

That meant the Comanches would be wanting
their rifles, and maybe even Wilson too!

Chapter Four

Leading his horse cautiously toward the faint odor of smoke, Long Runner halted at a place near one of the piñon pine trees. He studied the trampled snow, and the footprints of the men who had stopped here. His keen eyes took in every detail, his nose recognized the smell of damp coals and the fresh pine sap from the branches that had been broken. In spite of the waning moon and the falling snow which had begun to cover over the tracks, the events that took place here read like an open book to the Comanche scout.

Long Runner crossed the campsite, knelt by the dead fire, and held a hand over the blackened remains. His lips thinned and a frown deepened upon his face, lifting slightly at the corners. Leaning forward, he blew onto the coals, then fed a bit of tinder into them, expertly coaxing a small crackling blaze back to life.

In a moment the rest of the Comanches rode in from the shadows and circled around the fire. One by one they dismounted. Chilled to the bone, each brought a stick to the fire and soon a roaring blaze filled the little clearing above the dark ravine.

Broken Nose squatted by the fire and warmed his hands as his two dogs dashed off into the shadows. Long Runner hunkered down next to the chief and said, "There were three men here, and the wounded friend of Diego."

Broken Nose nodded. "They are not far ahead now."

Diego Beaubien bent over the fire, shivering. "What are you two talking about?"

Switching to Spanish, Broken Nose said, "The men who killed your brother are a short ride ahead of us."

Long Runner pointed to the tracks trailing down into the ravine, and at the other tracks leading away. "The man, Wilson, he is bad hurt. They stop here to make travois to carry him. When they finish, the men ride off that way."

"Making straight for Taos," Diego said.

Broken Nose and Long Runner nodded in agreement. Broken Nose said, "But they will not reach it ahead of us. With the wounded one with them, they will travel slow. Soon we will catch them and have the rifles."

"Rifles?" Diego barked, a scowl upon his face. "I don't give a damn about the rifles now, or the horses. It's *them* I want—the ones who killed Tomas." Diego strode away in anger.

Broken Nose and Long Runner remained near the fire, warming themselves as Diego walked a few dozen paces along the tracks leading south.

The wind had stopped blowing and now the night was so quiet that he could hear the fat snow drifting softly down around him. His hot, impatient breath hung in the icy air, as Diego hugged himself against the chill, staring into the blackness ahead. He thought of his brother and blinked back the sudden stinging at the corner of his eyes. They had been close all their lives—two orphans clinging to each other against a world turned angry toward them—as if it was their fault their mother and father were dead. As boys they had been inseparable. As men they had been not only brothers, but friends. Tomas, being the younger, had always gone along with Diego's schemes. He had looked up to Diego. He had trusted him . . . had trusted him with his life!

Diego's fists clenched, his knuckles feeling the sting of the frigid air. And now Tomas was dead, and the men responsible for it only a few hours ahead. Diego was anxious to be on his way. He glared back at the Comanches squatting around the fire. All they cared about was the rifles. Their urgency was different from his own.

Diego knew from years of trading with these Indians that the Comanches would do things in their own time. They could not be hurried if they did not wish to be. But he understood too that once Long Runner and Broken Nose were following a trail, little would shake them off of it.

It was useless trying to rush them, so Diego joined them at the fire until Broken Nose finally stood and gave the word to mount up.

Broken Nose whistled for the dogs. The two animals tromped in from the darkness, growling at each other over the carcass of a rabbit dangling from a bloodied muzzle. One of the dogs made a quick pass at Diego's leg, nipping at him. Diego kicked out, missed, and cursed the half-wild animals. Broken Nose merely grinned, gave the beasts an order in the Comanche tongue, and instantly they were at his side.

Diego despised the dogs. They were big, vicious, blood-hungry beasts. He'd have shot them long ago if he'd had his way about it. But that would likely have gotten his scalp lifted. Broken Nose delighted in the two animals. So Diego put up with them. The feeling was mutual, he knew. The dogs didn't like Diego either—they didn't like anyone who wasn't Comanche—but they put up with him.

Charles Bent had taken the lead, holding the reins to Wilson's horse, which dragged the travois carrying the wounded man. Hernando rode behind Wilson, sulking into the high collar of his coat, which he had turned up to cover his mouth and nose. Kit brought up the rear, his horse plodding forty feet or so behind the others, where he could hear better. The wind had died down, and on nights like this sound carried for great distances. Kit's senses were keen for anything out of the ordinary. He didn't know what he should be listening for, so every sound was important.

"So, tell me, Hernando, how did you get yourself mixed up with those *hombres*? How'd you come to be tied up in that tent?" Bent asked. "What did you try to steal from them?"

"A horse, *Señor* Bent. I was in need of a horse."

"So you decided just to take one of theirs?"

Hernando shrugged his shoulders. "It seemed a

good idea at the time. Only, it went very badly, I think."

"I'm surprised they didn't shoot you right off."

"They would have, if I had not told them about the gold."

"Pretty quick thinking."

"I was desperate."

"Well, desperation has a way of spurring a man on to quick thinking, I reckon," Bent noted dryly. "Who is this young lady that would make an otherwise honest man steal?"

"She is all that my heart has ever longed for, but her father is a heavy-handed *patrón* who thinks of only money. He would never allow his daughter to marry a poor man."

"So that is why you stole Don Francisco's gold?"

"It is not what I had wished to do, *Señor* Bent. But how else could a poor man such as myself ever acquire the wealth needed to make the old man change his mind about me?"

"Oh? So now you think he will look more favorably upon his daughter marrying a thief?"

Hernando glanced down. "It is not a thing I would have told him."

"How did you intend to explain eight hundred dollars in gold?"

He shrugged. "I did not consider that. Maybe I was a bit hasty, no?"

"I'd say you were a bit hasty, yes," Bent replied.

"It is love, *Señor* Bent. She makes a fool of every man."

"Well, you'll have plenty of time to ponder that while sitting in jail, Hernando."

Hernando stiffened upon the saddle. "Must it be so?"

"You made your bed, Hernando."

"If you get the gold back, perhaps you could let me just slip away, no?"

At the rear of the column, Kit had been listening with half an ear to the two of them talking. But Hernando's words just then caught his attention. "What do you mean *if* we get the gold back?"

The Mexican looked over his shoulder at the mountain man. "A poor choice of words, *Señor* Carson. Of course, I meant to say *when* you get the gold back." He gave Kit a toothy grin.

Bent said sternly, "The decision is not mine to make, Hernando. It was Don Francisco's gold you took and it will be up to Don Francisco to decide what to do with you."

Kit said, "I'm right curious about this mysterious woman. What sort of female could turn a man's head clear around? Who is she, anyway?"

Hernando's dark eyes took on a far-off glaze. "Ah, *Señor* Carson, she is the loveliest creature God ever did fashion for a man. Her hair is smooth as the finest silk, black as the coal taken from the ground. Her eyes shine as polished walnut shells, beaming with flecks of gold when the sunlight strikes upon them. One look from her and you become a slave to her beauty. A simple touch of her delicate hand is like water and food to a starving man. Honey flows from her tongue when she speaks! What else is there to say about such a woman, *Señor* Carson?"

Watching him with open amazement, Charlie Bent gave a long whistle and said, "Are you feeling all right, Hernando? Sure you haven't been standing out in the moonlight too long?"

Kit said, "Reckon I'd steal and kill for even half the woman he tells of."

Bent laughed. "I can see you've been bitten hard by this female. Does she have a name or do you intend to keep her identity all to yourself?"

"Lucky for you, Hernando, that Charlie just got himself hitched last week, or he just might take out after your young lady."

"It would be of no matter, *Señor* Carson," he responded confidently, "for it is me, Hernando Vigil, that she loves."

"I'm dying up here, Hernando. What's her name?"

Hernando smirked and said, "Maria Juanita Chacon."

Bent reined to a stop and turned back. "Come again?"

"Maria Juanita Chacon."

"Juan de Dios Chacon's third daughter?"

"*Sí*, the very one."

Bent tossed back his head and laughed.

"I see not what is so funny, *Señor* Bent," Hernando said peevishly.

"You know the gal?" Kit asked.

"I know her father well. And I've seen his daughters."

"Whal, is the filly all that Hernando makes out she is?"

"He told it straight enough, except he forgot to mention the fact that she's skinnier than a wagon tongue."

"She is slender as a willow!" Hernando countered.

"And she's got buck teeth."

"A smile that holds captive a man's heart!" Hernando insisted.

"And her feet—well, I've seen grizzly tracks more delicate."

"A good foundation! One not easily shaken by what fate throws at her!"

"All right, you two," Kit intervened. "I can see that you're both coming at this from different points of view and ain't likely to see eye-to-eye on the matter."

Hernando hunkered moodily down in his saddle, drawing himself deeper into his sheepskin coat. Charlie Bent chuckled and turned back to the trail ahead.

They were getting close to Arroyo Hondo, a long valley sparsely settled and famous for Simeon Turley's distillery and the Taos Lightning that he brewed mainly for the trappers who considered the traditional New Mexico drink of *aguardiente* a bit too mild. Kit didn't expect to see anyone up and about this late at night—early in the morning. He suspected that Charlie would ride right through the sleeping valley without stopping.

And that's exactly what he did.

Pausing atop a ridge beyond the valley, Kit wished the snow would stop falling so that he could get a glimpse of the stars and an idea of the time. It was nearing dawn, of that he was certain; perhaps an hour more before the first hints of it would tinge the eastern sky, definitely no more than two.

Kit looked back and a shiver suddenly gripped his sturdy frame. He grimaced, knowing that the feeling had nothing to do with the cold.

Bent reined to a stop when he noticed that Kit

had fallen behind. Handing over Wilson's horse to Hernando, Bent galloped back.

"What's wrong, Kit?"

"I don't know. I seem to have developed an itch I can't scratch." He glanced down the way they had come.

Bent's view traveled back along the trail they were leaving in the snow. "You've been living away from civilization too long, my friend. This isn't the wilds of the Rocky Mountains."

Kit gave a wry smile. "Maybe you're right."

"We'll be back in Taos in another four or five hours—say, you know what today is?"

"Christmas Eve day."

"And your birthday," Bent added.

Kit grinned. "You remembered."

"Of course I remembered, Kit. How could I forget a birthday that falls on such a notable day?"

The grin grew into a smile. It pleased Kit that the day hadn't escaped everyone's notice. Having a birthday that fell right before Christmas had been a lifelong frustration. The event was always being overshadowed by the greater birth celebrated the next day. Not that a birthday was anything to get very excited about—except when Kit considered the alternative—not like it had been when he was a boy. But sometimes Kit felt it would have been nice to have been born on a different day—one he did not have to share.

Chapter Five

The small company trudged on through the snowy night, weaving among the short-growth forest of piñon that blanketed the rolling foothills along the Sangre de Cristo Mountains. Seth Wilson had regained consciousness, and with it his vile temper. He cursed Kit for having shot him, cursed Bent for guiding the travois over the rockiest ground he could find, and cursed Hernando for ever having shown up at their hidden camp. He didn't seem to consider that if they had not tried to kill the Mexican, then changed their minds and kept him captive in the hopes of acquiring more gold, none of this might have happened to him and his partners.

Bent ignored the man's railing complaints and went right on searching out the rockiest trail through the trees. Hernando seemed particularly quiet about the whole affair, trying his best to ignore the raging invalid.

Kit had other things on his mind. Try as he might, he couldn't quite shake the feeling that they were not alone, that somewhere nearby danger lurked. It was nothing he could put a finger on. An odd sensation in his spine, a stiffening of the hairs at the back of his neck, a sudden clarity of hearing that made him aware of every sound in the dark forest; the distant hoot of an owl, a nearby coyote calling to its mate, a crack of a twig that might have been caused by a branch over-burdened with snow . . . or might not have been.

Finally Kit could stand it no longer. He reined to a stop and his eyes compressed slightly as he listened, fingers tightening around the long J. J. Henry rifle across his saddle. Up ahead Charlie Bent brought the little caravan again to a halt and looked back.

"Something the matter, Kit?"

"It's that itch, Charlie."

"Fixing on scratching it this time?"

Kit nodded. "I think I'll double back and take a look."

Bent snorted a long breath that hung momentarily in the cold air. "Well, I won't question your judgment in these matters. You've spent more time keeping your scalp off of an Indian lodge pole than I have."

"It's all that easy living you've been practicing these last few years, Charlie."

Bent laughed. "I finally figured out after enough cold and hungry years that trapping beaver and fighting Indians was not the road to wealth I'd been led to believe it was when my brother-in-law, Lilburn, took me with him to join up with Lisa's company."

"Whal, you always were a mite smarter than me, Charlie."

Bent laughed again. "We'll wait here for you. Don't be long or I might commence to worrying."

Seth Wilson had been listening to all of this. He shifted a bloodshot eye at Bent and growled, "I'm shot to pieces and bleeding like a pig, Bent. You need to get me to a doctor!"

"You aren't shot to pieces, you've only got a few busted ribs. And you aren't bleeding to death either, but if you keep making a fuss you're liable to be." Bent waved Kit on his away. "Go and scratch that itch. We'll be waiting here for you when you get back."

Kit turned his horse away and in a few minutes Bent and the others were out of sight. Alone, he retraced the trail they had left in their wake, his ears alert for any sound out of the usual, his sharp blue eyes probing the recesses of the shadowy landscape. After a dozen minutes of this, Kit angled his horse to the left and paralleled the tracks in the snow, far enough off the trail that anyone coming up it would not immediately spot him.

Not that he fully expected that there would be anyone.

But whenever he got that particular itch, that creeping across his hide which came at the most unexpected times, Kit knew it was dangerous not to take another look over his shoulder. Charles Bent accused him of having lived in the wilds too long.

Maybe yes, maybe no.

All Kit knew for sure was that after almost ten years in this land of towering mountains, burning deserts, freezing winters, and unpredictable Indians, he was still alive and in possession of his scalp. And that was more than could be said about most of the men who had come west following the beaver trail.

A rustling in the trees behind him brought him instantly around in his saddle, his rifle leveled. An owl leaped skyward and flapped heavily above the tops of the low piñons. Kit eased off the trigger and let go of a caught breath. A tight grin spread across his face. Giving a gentle tap of his heels, he urged his horse forward.

Keeping an eye on the trail to his right, Kit briefly considered the two dead men he had left behind in the arroyo, wondering who they were. If they had not reached for their guns, could he have bargained for Hernando? He would have preferred that to the showdown. It was never a pleasant thing to take another man's life, even when the only choices left to you were kill or be killed. Once done, a killing could never be completely forgotten, regardless of the circumstances. But a man does what he has to do to survive, and he lives with the consequences. If you couldn't, you had no business being here.

But *Comancheros* and Comanches were only two of the many dangers he had to be on the lookout for. This country was thick with mountain lions and wolves, and even a bear or two this late in the season was not unheard-of.

Another dozen minutes passed. Kit hunkered deeper into his shaggy buffaloskin coat. His horse plodded on. Snow drifted down all around him, crunched softly under his horse's hooves, fell like little landslides off heavily laden pine boughs.

Kit was beginning to think that all his precautions had been unnecessary. He'd left his friends back there in the cold to wait for him, and so far he had found no danger. All this time they could have been on their way to Taos. With a wry grin, he thought that maybe Charles Bent had been right. Maybe he had spent too many years outside the numbing influence of the civilized world, with its safe cities and helpful neighbors, and town constables whose job it was to see that peace was maintained.

Thinking it over, Kit was hard put to remember a time when he had lived any other way. His father had gone west with the frontiersmen and borderers long before civilized society had followed on his tracks. Kit had never known any other life than the one he was living now; the kind where a man took care of his own troubles in whatever way he could, be it with guns, fists, knives, or quick thinking and smooth words. There had never been a time in his life, except when he was very young, when he could count on someone else looking out for him.

And Kit liked it that way!

Suddenly his horse's ears cocked forward. Kit drew rein and peered hard ahead, ears straining. Nothing moved in the darkness, no sounds to indicate what was out there, but his horse had heard something, even if he hadn't.

"Get down off that horse, Hernando. I don't want to have to worry from one minute to the next that you're trying to sneak off again."

"*Señor* Bent, I would never do that." Hernando's voice was a mixture of dismay and shock, and perhaps even a little disappointment too.

Bent shot the Mexican a skeptical stare.

"Besides, where could I go where you or *Señor* Carson could not come and take me back?"

Bent beat himself with his arms to drive away some of the cold. He tied the animals to a branch and set his rifle against a nearby rock.

From the litter, Seth Wilson watched as Bent blew into his fists to warm his hands.

"How long are we gonna wait here?" Wilson demanded.

Bent glanced up. "Until Kit gets back."

"I'm freezing. How about a fire?"

"We won't be that long, Wilson." Bent shoved his hands deep into the pocket of his coat and walked a few paces down the trail, peering off in the distance. He looked back at the man on the litter and said, "Besides, if there *is* someone sniffing our trail, I wouldn't want to advertise our presence with a fire and wood smoke in the air."

Wilson's eyes compressed. A plan began to take shape. He glanced at Hernando, who was presently making a steaming yellow hole in the snow. Hernando didn't want to go back any more than he did. Perhaps there was something there he could use; an ally in the skinny Mexican, maybe? In spite of the cold and the wound in his side, Wilson was not nearly as bad off as he wanted Bent and Carson to believe. The bleeding had stopped, and he had suffered through broken ribs before. The torn muscle and flesh hurt most, but it was nothing compared to the burning hatred that flared within him toward Kit Carson. Twice now the man had put a bullet in him. Carson would pay for that. One way or another, Carson would pay!

Lying on this litter without even a knife, he was practically helpless. Somehow he had to get his hands on a weapon. . . . His thoughts came to a halt and his eyes shifted back toward Bent as the plan suddenly became clear. Pressing a hand upon his wound, Wilson let out a long moan.

Bent glanced back over his shoulder.

Wilson said, "I think it is started bleeding again, Bent. I'm hurting real bad."

"There isn't anything I can give you for the pain until we get back to Taos."

"I won't make it to Taos, Bent. I'll bleed to death long before then." Wilson bellowed out another groan and seemed to pass out.

Hernando wandered over to the litter and peered down at Wilson. He turned a worried face toward Charlie Bent. "Is he dying, *Señor* Bent?"

Exasperated, Bent strode back to the litter. "I don't see how he could be. But I reckon I'd better take another look at that wound just the same. Kit will have my hide if I let this *hombre* up and die on him before he has a chance to get him back to the States."

"Maybe he will not be too upset," Hernando noted.

Bent grinned. "A bit of insight there, Hernando?"

The Mexican shrugged. "I think *Señor* Carson feels a duty to the *señorita*'s father, that is all. If this man were to die, maybe it would be a relief to him, no? But why ask me, *Señor* Bent? I am but a poor *peón*. I know very little."

"Hmm. I'm not so sure about that."

Wilson felt Bent open the buttons of his coat,

letting in a flood of cold air. He groaned softly, pretending to be unconscious when he felt the man's fingers upon his blood-soaked shirt. Bent leaned over him for a closer look.

"It doesn't appear to be bleeding at all," he said to Hernando.

"Maybe on the inside, where it does not show?" Hernando suggested.

"I don't think so."

Wilson parted an eye, and, seeing his opportunity, he carefully slipped his hand under Bent's coat. But before he could grab the pistol he had seen Bent put there, Bent moved. Wilson only just managed to withdraw his hand before the businessman went around the travois to look at the wound from that angle.

"It's not bleeding," he said impatiently. "And I don't want to hear another word about it until we get back to Taos."

Wilson felt the icy night air being closed off as Bent buttoned up the coat again. Through slitted eyes he watched Bent walk back to the rock, take up his rifle, and blow the snow from its nipple.

Silently Wilson cursed himself for his foiled attempt, but there would be another time, he promised himself, another chance at that pistol. And that next time he'd not fail!

Hernando trailed after the merchant, beating his arms to flog away the cold and get the blood moving again. "*Señor* Bent," he said, "if somehow you had Don Francisco Jaramillo's gold back right now, held it in your hand, could you not maybe turn your back on me for a little while?"

"You're asking me again to let you go free?"

Hernando nodded.

Bent frowned. "I can't do that."

"But why not, if you were to have the gold back? What difference could it make to you? I would go far away, and I would never steal again."

Bent cocked a doubtful eye in his direction. "You expect me to believe that, Hernando?"

Hernando flashed him a lame smile.

"I thought so. I already told you, it's Don Francisco's place to decide what to do with you." Bent's view narrowed suddenly. "Is the gold hidden nearby, Hernando? Is that why you're asking me this?"

Hernando's long, saddened face peered out at him from the fleecy collar of his sheepskin coat. "Sí, the gold, she is nearby."

"Well, good. Just as soon as Kit gets back we'll go and fetch it." Bent laid the rifle back against the rock and warmed his hands with his breath. His eyes went to the trampled tracks, which were already beginning to fill with snow, watching for his friend's return.

Wilson watched too. He would get another chance at Bent's pistol, and when he did, it would be Kit Carson on the taking end of the gun, and he'd be on the giving end.

Chapter Six

Kit urged his horse farther off the trail, and for a long moment the mountain man did not move, his gaze fixed ahead. He knew well that a horse's hearing was better than any human's. A horse could recognize the approaching footsteps of his owner long before a human could ever detect that someone was coming. And Kit's horse had just heard something. More than once the twitch in a horse's ear or an uncertain break in an otherwise even gait had been warning enough to save a man's life. In this country, where seconds counted more than in most places, Kit had to rely on even the smallest of signs to survive. The men who had never learned to read the warnings on a gut level were the men who ended up being buried here.

At first all Kit heard was his own breathing, and the soft patter of snowflakes gently hitting his hat, his coat, and the pine trees all around him that hid him from view. Then suddenly, a few hundred feet down the trail, a bit of movement caught his eye. Slowly emerging from the shadows, the dark forms stood out against the white landscape. Although the intervening trees hampered Kit's view, he could see that the riders were bundled in buffalo robes, all except for one of the men at the head of the party. This one wore a wool coat, a black, flat-brim hat, and a scarf wrapped around his nose and mouth. The others were Indians—Comanches, Kit realized as they came nearer.

Kit placed a soothing hand against his horse's neck and whispered, "Hush. This is no time to get sociable."

The Indians were driving a herd of horses, fifteen or twenty. Through the trees, Kit couldn't be certain of the count. As the party drew up along the trail, Kit caught a glimpse of a dog—no, two dogs—sniffing the snow ahead of them.

His horse stomped and threw its head.

"Easy now," Kit breathed near the animal's ear.

It was as he had suspected. The men were *Comancheros*. And now they were on the trail of their wounded friend . . . and the men who had killed their partners. Kit had to get back to Bent and warn him before this trouble arrived.

Turning his horse, Kit quietly started away at an angle, hoping to put a healthy distance between himself and the band of Comanches.

Just then one of the *Comancheros'* horses whinnied.

Kit's animal tossed its head. Kit tugged at the reins to stop it from answering, but just the same it stomped and fought the bit.

Suddenly the wind shifted. Down on the trail,

the two dogs stopped dead in their tracks and pointed their noses toward him. Their ears flattened back against the sides of their heads and their lips drew back, showing teeth in the faint moonlight. With a sudden howl of excitement, they burst into motion, plunging through the snow straight for Kit.

Broken Nose brought the warriors to a halt. He had a puzzled look upon his face that was a mixture of curiosity and concern as he watched the dogs burst into a run and disappear into the dark pine forest. He sat astride his horse listening to the sounds of their excited chase growing more distant. Finally, after a minute had passed, Broken Nose called to the dogs, ordering them to return. But the savage barking only faded farther into the night.

"It is nothing," Diego said, irritated at Broken Nose's delay. Inwardly, he hoped the dogs had come upon the scent of a bear and were even now were being torn and shaken by the beast's massive jaws—just as so many times he had seen the half-wild dogs doing to their own prey.

Broken Nose ignored the Mexican, his dark eyes narrowing suspiciously. Again he called for the dogs to return. The barking only grew fainter.

"They will come back," Diego said, adding under his breath, "unfortunately."

Three of the Indians were busy keeping the loose horses bunched together, but the other warriors spoke among themselves in the Comanche tongue, of which Diego knew only a smattering. He sensed that they were nervous about the dogs' peculiar actions, but he couldn't understand why.

The dogs were forever dashing off this way and that, usually coming back with their muzzles bloodied and a fresh rabbit dangling in their powerful jaws. Then they would fight over the kill until one or the other gave it up. It was always like that. It would be like that this time too, Diego was certain.

Yet somehow, Broken Nose and his warriors were taking this incident differently.

"What is it?" Diego asked, his curiosity finally overcoming the impatient fire of revenge that burned within him toward those men responsible for his brother's murder.

With his eyes compressed and his mouth a tight, worried knot, Broken Nose suddenly turned to his warriors and barked a command. Instantly three men broke rank and rode after the dogs.

Diego threw up his hands in disgust at the delay. But the Indians would have their way, and all he could do was wait for them to satisfy their curiosity. He was certain the dogs would be returning any second.

But this time they did not.

In spite of all his caution, Kit had been discovered. He flung a curse at the fidgety horse beneath him while at the same time yanking its head around and driving his heels into its flanks. The animal leaped into motion, plunging recklessly through the dense pine growth.

Pounding along the uneven ground, Kit had all he could do to keep from being swept out of the saddle by the passing pine boughs. He held the reins in his left hand and clung to the long rifle with his right, trying to keep it from being yanked from his fist by the branches.

He cast a quick glance over his shoulder. He didn't see the dogs at once, but their growing barks told Kit they were drawing nearer. His horse was having difficulty in the snow, its flying hooves coming down on snow-buried sticks and rocks that broke its gait and caused it to stumble along the sloping ground.

The forest floor took a steep dive, and his horse tucked in its rear legs, plowing its way to the bottom of the ravine, where it scrambled for footing once again and veered right, following the twisting, dropping course of another dark ravine. In the shadows behind him, Kit caught a glimpse of two dark forms leaping down the slope he'd just negotiated. Without a break in their stride, they shot toward him, like arrows streaking across the ground, legs pumping, tails flying straight out behind them; spending more time soaring through the air, it seemed, than actually touching the ground.

Kit formed these impressions in a series of quick glances, stolen when he wasn't otherwise trying to see where his horse was carrying him, ducking the low branches that grabbed out at him from the dark. The savage barking grew louder, merging now with the thunder of his horse's hooves and the pounding blood in his ears. He knew then that he would not be able to outrun these dogs, and the last thing he wanted to do was to try to fight them.

But then fate took the decision out of his hands.

A piñon pine tilting out of the side of the arroyo loomed suddenly before him. Kit leaned far to the left, but there just wasn't enough room. The horse ducked its head and the heavy, snow-laden bough smacked him in the chest, batting Kit out of the saddle and dumping its burden of snow upon him as he sprawled spread-eagle upon the ground.

The impact drove his breath out of him. His rifle flew away into the shadows as the horse galloped onward into the night, following the dark twistings and turnings of the small canyon. Stunned, all Kit wanted to do was lie there gasping for air. But time was not something he had much of. The barking dogs were almost upon him. Fighting off the paralyzing weight that enveloped him and crushed the air from his lungs, Kit managed to brush some of the snow from his coat. He ripped open the horn buttons holding the buffaloskin closed and his hand dove inside for the big butcher knife there. But the knife had twisted around in the fall and was caught between his back and the ground.

For the first time since his flight began, a touch of panic grabbed hold of Kit. He grappled at its hilt, fighting to free the knife from beneath him. His eyes expanded as the first of the furry missiles launched itself at his throat.

Then the blade came free of the sheath. Drawing it out, Kit had only a moment to fling an arm across his neck to protect his throat and thrust the knife up at the growling fury that had filled the field of his vision. Somehow, his aim was perfect, and as the dog descended upon him, the point of Kit's knife found its breastbone. It was not so much Kit's doing as it was the downward force of the attacking dog that drove the blade into the breastbone, clear to the hilt.

The dog's momentum carried it onward, but the animal was dead even before it crashed into the snow a few inches beyond Kit's head.

The second dog sprang for Kit's jugular. Kit attempted to pull the knife back, but the blade had lodged deep in the bone, and was impossible to remove. All he could do was throw an arm in front of him and feel the powerful jaws crush down on the buffaloskin. If it hadn't been for the heavy coat, the dog's attack would have nearly severed his wrist. As it was, the sharp fangs punctured the thick hide and found the softer skin beneath, where they tasted blood. Kit ignored the pain. His free hand wrapped around the dog's powerful neck. Its fur was so thick Kit could hardly get a grip around it, but he did, and he managed to hook his thumb into the animal's windpipe.

The dog thrashed its head back and forth as if trying to shake the life from a bird it had just captured. Kit knew that if he let the animal slip from his grasp, it would be his throat that would be between those deadly jaws next. Kit squeezed with all his strength, but it seemed to have little effect upon the enraged beast. The dog just clamped down tighter and twisted more violently, its claws digging at the coat as if it had in mind to excavate a hole in which to bury a bone . . . or a hand.

Kit's difficult breathing didn't help any. In his condition he could not hang onto the animal much longer. The dog was a hundred pounds of muscle and teeth, seemingly impossible to stop, and wanting only one thing, to thrash the life out of him. Kit had to free his other hand. Twisting it

Doug Hawkins

within the sleeve, he felt the dog's teeth working on the buffalo hide like a machine, seeking out flesh and blood. Gritting back the pain, he pulled his arm, feeling his flesh tear. Then he was free of the relentless teeth which still gnawed at the sleeve, slavering on it, not caring that Kit's wrist was no longer inside it. The dog had tasted Kit's blood there and that was enough to keep it grinding away, growling, throwing its head back and forth, trying to rip the sleeve to shreds, and at the same time trying to free its neck from Kit's grasp.

Slowly the beast was shaking itself out of Kit's fingers; Kit's grip upon its throat was weakening. Kit struggled to work his arm out of the sleeve. If his strength should fail him now—if he lost his grip on that shaggy neck, with one arm trapped inside his coat—it would be all over in seconds. In spite of the icy air, Kit was sweating rivulets from under the wolfskin hat; perspiration that made glistening tracks down his cheek.

As if it had finally realized that there was no arm in the sleeve anymore, the dog suddenly released the mauled buffalo hide and strove at Kit's throat. Its hot breath was only inches from Kit's cheek while its wild, bared teeth and ear-numbing bark slobbered saliva all over the mountain man's face. Tucking his elbow, Kit pulled his right arm free of the sleeve. He grabbed at the pistol tucked under his belt, and got a fist around it.

The dog snapped out. A fang opened a gash in Kit's cheek. Kit's finger's weakened. No longer holding the dog's throat, he desperately clung to the thick fur. But even that was slipping through his weakening fingers. It was only a matter of seconds before the animal would shake itself completely free of him. In those remaining seconds, Kit tilted the pistol under the heavy coat, pressed it against the dog's chest, fought with the hammer, which had caught in the material of his shirt, cocked it, and yanked the trigger.

The weapon exploded, muffled by the coat and the dog. Kit felt the heat of the blast through his shirt. The dog let out a single yelp, yet kept snapping at his face as blood spurted from the bullet wound. But the animal quickly weakened and, mustering all his remaining strength, Kit flung it off him. Lying in the snow with its four legs kicking as if within its tortured brain it imagined itself chasing a rabbit, the panting dog whimpered. Its tongue lolled into the snow, and blood spurted from the chest wound with each beat of its failing heart, turning the white snow red.

Kit groaned and pushed himself upright, wincing at the stab of pain from his back. He examined his right hand, which still grasped the pistol. Blood flowed freely from a half dozen puncture wounds, but luckily not one of them had ripped an artery. Wearily, he stood, cradling his hand. He took a rag from his hunting bag and wrapped it as tightly about his hand as he could. The pain stiffened his fingers and swelled up his arm. Grimacing, Kit buttoned his coat against the chill night air and reached down for his knife, putting a foot upon the dog and giving a mighty yank. Every muscle in his back cried out and his lungs drew in fire with each breath. The knife came free and Kit wiped the blood upon the dog's fur.

He staggered, and stabbed a foot out to catch himself. Looking around the bloodied ground, he spied his rifle lying a few feet away, and went stiffly to it, wincing again as he bent to snatch it up from the snow. He blew on the nipple and saw that the cap had been knocked off in the fall. Awkwardly, with his left hand, he dug his capper from the pouch, pressed the button, and snapped a fresh cap onto the nipple. Carefully, Kit lowered the hammer onto it, then drew it back to the first notch.

The sound of approaching horses turned his head toward the place where his horse had slid down into the ravine. The movement sent a stinging wave of pain up his neck. Every muscle in his body seemed to ache. The hoofbeats became louder, and a moment later the first of the Comanches started down the slope.

"Damnation!"

Wheeling about in the opposite direction, Kit started up the wall of the ravine. The Comanches were far enough away that they did not immediately see him. Kit scrambled up the rocky incline, leaving bloody prints where his right hand clawed at the snow. No matter how hard he tried, Kit knew he would never get away without leaving a clear trace for them to follow. And he didn't even try to hide his escape.

He reached the top and started off in a dog trot that jarred every nerve in his body. It was without a doubt one helluva way to be spending one's birthday, he groused.

And he wondered just then if this might not be his last!

Chapter Seven

One by one the Comanches dismounted and tromped around the clearing, trying to work some heat into their bodies. Breaking off into small groups, they spoke softly among themselves as they waited, filling the air with the gray clouds of their breath. Every now and then a distant sound would bring a sudden silence to the clearing as the men stopped to listen. Afterwards, when the sound had been identified, their low mumblings would start up again.

Diego Beaubien only caught snatches of the several different conversations, but he gathered that the general topic of discussion was what had delayed the three riders whom Broken Nose had sent after the dogs, and what was it the dogs had sensed in the first place? An animal or a man? The warriors were pretty evenly divided over that last question—Diego had learned that last bit of information from Broken Nose himself, who gave it to him in Spanish.

"How long are we to wait here, Broken Nose?"

The Indian was becoming annoyed at Diego's insistence to be on their way. "We stay until I say we leave."

It was not wise to antagonize the Comanches. Diego inclined his head at the dark trees where the dogs and riders had disappeared. "When they get back you will see it was nothing. A jackrabbit, that's all."

Diego strode back to his horse, disgusted. Because of a rabbit, the men who had killed Tomas might escape his vengeance. But there was little he could do to change the stubborn Comanche's mind once it was set upon a matter—even if that matter was only waiting for two half-wild dogs to come romping back after their frolic!

The Comanches weren't the only ones waiting. A few miles to the north, Charles Bent leaned against the rock where his rifle rested, hugging what little warmth remained within his coat. On the litter, Seth Wilson had begun to shiver, and Bent suspected that unless they reached Taos soon, the cold just might accomplish what Kit's bullet had failed to do. Somehow, he didn't think Kit would be overly disappointed if Wilson did freeze to death. Like Hernando had said, taking Wilson back to Missouri was an obligation Kit felt he still owed the father of the girl Wilson had ravaged. But a letter to the man telling of Wilson's capture and death might serve just as well. And it would entail a lot less effort.

Hernando was standing near the horses, stomping his feet and flailing his arms across himself. Bent could not remember a colder night, and he longed for Don Francisco's warm house, or his own little adobe home, which he had built not far from his new bride's father. Although he and his brother, William, operated the big adobe trading house on the Arkansas River, of late Charles had taken up residence in Taos, where he and his business partner, Cerean St. Vrain, had opened a store on the south side of the plaza. Now that Bent had acquired a wife and a four-year-old daughter, Rumalda, it looked as though he would be spending a lot more time in Taos, rooting himself deeper into the hard, red earth of this Mexican community.

Bent sighed out a cloud of steam. He missed his new bride, Ignacia, and yes, he missed Taos too. Once again, for perhaps the hundredth time, Bent peered down the tracks, which had nearly filled with fresh snow.

Wilson shifted on the litter and let out a low groan. "I'm freezing here, Bent," he growled. "Let's get a move on. That bastard Carson will catch up. He could trail a mountain goat up the side of Pike's Peak if he wanted to. I know that firsthand."

"If I had a blanket I'd give it to you. When Kit and I set off after Hernando this morning, we had no idea we'd be out all night. Didn't think to bring any." Bent considered a moment, then said, "But I know of something that might help." He went to Wilson's horse and began working at the knots that held the litter to the saddle. As he did so he caught a glimpse of Hernando slowly leading one of the horses away. Bent swung back for his rifle and the sound of the heavy hammer being drawn back rang in the air.

Hernando stopped at once, his back going as rigid as the raked masts of a Baltimore Clipper.

"Fixing to take that animal to grass again, Hernando?" Bent's voice was easygoing, but it held a razor-sharp edge of warning.

The Mexican grinned over his shoulder and laughed. "*Sí, Señor* Bent, but maybe that is not so good an idea?"

"Not so good," Bent agreed. "I think it's time I tie you up, Hernando."

"No, please. I will not take the horses to feed again."

"No you won't, Hernando, because the next time you try to sneak away from me will be your last time, *amigo*."

Hernando tied the horse back to the tree branch and came sheepishly toward Bent. "You joke, yes? You would not shoot, would you?"

"I joke *no*," Bent answered. "I will shoot. I reckon a bullet through your right kneecap will keep you from wandering away anymore."

Hernando shivered, staring at the rifle in Bent's fist. "I think I will stay by that rock there," he said.

"That would be a very good idea."

Hernando anchored himself at the rock while Charles Bent unsaddled Wilson's horse, pulled off the saddle blanket, and spread it over Wilson.

"Reckon this is the best I can do for you, Wilson."

Bent resaddled Wilson's horse and tied the travois back in place. Then he strolled a few feet off and stared out into the night. "What the devil is keeping Kit anyway? He's been gone almost an hour."

"*Señor* Bent?"

He wheeled back toward the Mexican. "What is it?"

"When I was tied up inside their tent, I overheard some of the words they were speaking."

"What did you hear?"

"There was talk about some other men. They were waiting for them, I think. I heard a name spoken. Diego, I think it was."

Bent's view shifted momentarily toward the crates of rifles. "Waiting for them? So, someone was coming for the rifles. What else did you hear?"

Hernando shrugged his shoulders. "Only that there was some mention of horses. I think they were waiting for horses too. That is all I remember. My brain, it was all whirling around. I was afraid they would kill me."

"Shut up, you greaser. We should have killed you right off. If it weren't for that second bag of gold—" Wilson's words broke off in anger.

Bent glared at Wilson. "Second bag of gold? What are you talking about?"

"Nothing."

Bent looked at Hernando. The Mexican gave him a silly grin and another shrug.

"There is something I'm not being told, Hernando."

"*Señor* Bent, would I keep secrets from such a fair and wise *patrón* as yourself? My good friend?" He grinned widely.

"Hernando, you're full of horseshit. What did he mean about a second bag of gold?"

"Nothing, I am sure."

"Wilson?"

The wounded man glared back at Bent. "The greaser had a bag of gold on him. We took it from him and we would have killed him too, but he said he had another bag hidden away somewhere. So we kept his mangy hide alive so's he could show us where it was."

"You took one bag from him?"

"I just said I did—well, Tomas took it."

"One of the men Kit killed."

Wilson's silence was answer enough. "Where is this bag of gold?" Bent demanded.

"Hell if I know. I was unconscious when you rode up, or have you forgotten that? Tomas had the gold last time I seen it. Maybe he still has it."

"I checked the bodies before we left. There was no gold on either one . . ." Bent suddenly shifted his glare. "Hernando?"

"Me?"

"I don't see any other lying, thieving ingrates about. You were rummaging the pockets of one of those dead men. I saw you."

"I only wanted to discover who they were, so we could inform their families, that is all."

Bent held out a hand.

Hernando stared at it, a blank and innocent look upon his face.

Bent's rifle snapped up and leveled at the Mexican's nose.

Hernando grimaced and reached into a pocket. Reluctantly, he deposited Don Francisco Jaramillo's pouch of gold coins into Bent's hand. He grinned sheepishly. "What are you going to do to me now?"

"I ought to skin you alive and feed you to the

wolves, Hernando. How could you steal from a man who has practically treated you like a son?"

"I already told you. It is love, *Señor* Bent! What man would not steal for one so lovely as my Juanita Chacon? The sun rises in her eyes, the wilting cactus rose draws strength from her touch, and the very words from her red lips—"

"Yeah, I know. You already told me. Her words flow like honey. Hernando, I'm really disappointed in you."

"I am sorry, *Señor* Bent." He lowered his eyes regretfully, but still managed to keep Bent's face in view.

Bent snorted his disgust. "Get back over there by that rock and stay put this time. If you try sneaking off again, I swear I'll shoot first and ask what you were about afterwards."

Hanging his head, Hernando walked back and, sinking farther into his heavy coat, he wrapped his arms about himself and stared at his boots.

Bent gave another snort, glanced at the pouch, then shoved it into his coat pocket and went back to watching for Kit's return.

Moving helped . . . a little.

If he had lain still when he had fallen from his horse—if the dogs had not forced him to immediately use his muscles—he'd have been as stiff as winter molasses about now. But the life and death struggle, and now his jogging away from the ravine with a band of Comanche warriors on his trail, did wonders for limbering his back, neck, and shoulders. His strained muscles hurt, no denying that, but at least they hadn't seized up on him as he had feared they might. Kit had been extremely fortunate that the fall hadn't broken something important, and he reckoned the hand of Providence, and a cushion of freshly fallen snow, had something to do with his narrow escape.

But he wasn't out of the woods yet. . . .

A wry grin creased his face as his brain turned over that fitting expression. Slipping noiselessly past the piñon pines that crowded in on him from all sides, Kit listened for the sounds of pursuit coming from behind him. It had been several minutes, and he knew that by now the Comanches had discovered the two dogs, and the bloody signs of the battle. And he knew too, that in not very many more minutes the Indians would be following the clear trail he was leaving behind in the deep snow.

Through the fog of his own breath, Kit spied a wall of rock rising from the forest floor to his right. Veering toward it, he quickly surveyed the place, considering whether this was a good enough position for a man to make a stand. Kit still didn't know how many Comanches would be coming after him. He had seen only one, but he was certain more were following right behind him. But whether it was two or ten, he could never outrun them, and he couldn't hide his tracks. The battle would come sooner or later, and Kit would rather have it sooner, from a place of his choosing, rather than later, on the run and in the open.

His hand was throbbing, the pain beginning to mask the ache in every muscle that ran up his back into his neck. At least his breathing was slowly coming back to normal, and it no longer felt as if he had inhaled a lump of burning coal. Kit forced himself to flex his fingers. He could not allow the hand to go stiff on him, not right now.

Circling the outcropping of rock, Kit saw that it was more massive than he'd first guessed. It stabbed up through the trees like a giant fang, and in one place folded back on itself—as if the fang had developed a cavity. Kit slipped into the fold and found a handhold. A stab of pain drew back his lips as he slowly pulled himself up into the rock and worked his way to a ledge that climbed steeply. At a spot where he had a view of the forest below, Kit stopped and squeezed back into a deep cleft.

Hunkering down in the shadows, he quickly reloaded his pistol. It was not an easy task. His right hand barely worked, and when he cocked the hammer to gently lower it back in place, it nearly slipped out from under his thumb and almost discharged the weapon. He frowned as he fitted the pistol to his palm, wincing as he forced his fingers to close around it. The mauled hand would work after a fashion, but it did not work very well. He slipped the pistol back under his belt and checked the second one, which was still loaded and capped.

Then he unwrapped the cloth from his hand and examined the wounds. The bleeding had slowed. Some of the shallower punctures had begun to crust over, and the others were on their way. Holding his rifle between his knees, Kit sat back to wait for the Indians to come.

He didn't have long to wait. They appeared suddenly and silently from the trees below. Kit pressed back into the cleft and watched first one, then two riders appear between the trees. A moment later a third rider came out of the shadows off to one side. They stopped, studying Kit's tracks, then lifted their eyes to the tall rock before them.

Even though he knew that they could not see him, Kit's skin crawled as their searching eyes scanned the rocky outcropping, probing the deep shadows where he had hidden himself. Kit held his breath, not wanting the steam of it to give away his position. He knew they would circle around behind the rock next. They would rightly guess that this outcropping would be the place for a man on the run to turn and make a stand. They'd be wary of an attack. They'd surely find the fissure where Kit had climbed the crag. And then they would find him.

Chapter Eight

As Kit suspected they might, the Comanches split up and slowly started circling the rock, approaching it from either side. Kit's body tingled in anticipation of the coming fight. At least now he knew how many there were. Only three of them. There could have been a dozen. Still, even in the best of health, Kit did not relish the thought of facing three Comanches single-handedly. And Kit's health at the moment was a little shy of being in top form.

His quickened heartbeat sent a surge of blood through his veins that numbed the pain in his hand and the injured muscles across his back, giving him renewed vigor. He was only mildly relieved that none of the Indians carried a rifle. Just the same, the Comanches were right handy with bows and arrows, and these three had theirs in hand, with arrows already nocked in the bowstrings.

When the Indians had moved beyond his view, Kit crept out onto the ledge and discovered that it ended abruptly a few feet farther on. At the tips of his moccasins, the rock angled sharply to the ground. Kit guessed it was a twelve-foot drop, maybe more. He glanced up at the rock tip soaring overhead. Short of sprouting wings, there was no way that he was going to climb that. He turned back. The way he had come was the only way left to go, and in a few minutes that would be filled with Comanches.

Hunkering down to listen to the whispered sounds of their voices now coming from the cleft in the rock, Kit knew they had found the way up, and they had found him.

His thoughts raced ahead. What would he do in their place? The last thing he'd do is follow a wounded grizzly into its den ... without first looking the place over real carefully. After all, a treed coon is going to remain a treed coon until he is dragged down from its branches. Kit heard a noise below and quickly backed into the deeper shadows again, going rigid to blend in with the dark rock around him. He held his rifle perfectly still and breathed shallowly into the collar of his coat to hide the steam from his breath. No sooner had he done so than one of the Comanches appeared below, stalking a slow circle around the rock, peering intently up at it.

Kit could have put a bullet through the man's heart in a eye-blink, but that would have surely alerted the other Indians whom he had seen with the herd of horses. And Kit certainly didn't need any more than three Comanches hounding his trail. For the moment, all he could do was keep motionless. His bruised and strained muscles were stiffening, and he felt an urgent need to stretch them. But he dared not move. The frozen rock pressing hard against his back was slowly probing through the thick buffalohide coat with its icy fingers. Kit pulled his hands up into the coat's shaggy sleeves to try to warm them some.

The Indian below continued his slow, cautious circuit, moving out of sight beyond the shoulder of the rock. Remaining as still as an icicle worked again, but sooner or later their suspicion would give at least one of those bucks the courage to climb up into this rock and check it out personally.

Kit let go of a breath and shifted upon his haunches. A sound to his left grabbed his attention and turned his head. It was a soft scraping against rock. Just as he suspected, one of the Indians had already started up into the cleft.

Creeping into the bear's den, are you? Kit mused, tightening his fist around the rifle.

Two of the Comanches reappeared below, taking a second turn around the rock. They knew he was up there. It was just a matter of flushing him out. And their bird dog was on his way up to see to the matter. Kit would have liked to have been able to think of a way out without a fight, but it didn't look like that was to be. Even so, he was determined to manage it without using a rifle or a pistol; without alerting the others . . . if he could.

As the two men below moved out of sight once again, Kit shifted his grip on his rifle, grimacing at the pain in his right hand. There was hardly room on the narrow ledge of rock for any sort of fight, and that meant a swift, surprise attack on his part. He reckoned he could easily take care of a lone man. But in doing so he would expose his position to the two Indians still below.

The bird dog would have done his job.

The bear would be in the open. Could it be helped? If so, Kit didn't know how.

The soft scraping sound grew louder. Kit braced himself. The two Indians below were still somewhere out of sight. On the far side of this huge rock, Kit hoped, probing the deep shadows to catch a glimpse of him. At least he had one element of surprise left to him: the lone Comanche on his way up did not yet know that the ledge ended only a few feet beyond. If he had, he might have peered more carefully into the dark fissure to his left. Instead he gave it a passing glance then crept past it, his hunched figure silhouetted starkly against the gray moonlit snow beyond.

Kit made his move. The Comanche heard the sound of Kit lashing forward, but he was too slow in mounting a defense. Kit snapped the butt of his rifle up and into the man's gut, buckling him over. He teetered there on the edge. Kit hooked a heel into the Indian's chest and sent him sailing out over the brink to a bone-crunching landing a dozen feet below. Kit looked down. The Comanche didn't move; his neck and back were twisted unnaturally around.

There had been hardly any noise—the thump at the end of the Indian's fall being the most of it. But it wasn't over, not with two more somewhere below. And Kit knew that they would not be so easy to get at.

The two Comanches circled into view again.

One of them spied the man lying in a heap and both rushed over. In a moment they would figure out what had happened, and once they did, the fissure would not offer Kit a second chance. He glanced at their horses, calculated his chances, knew it was now or never, and made his break.

Kit hardly felt the cold as he lurched from the crevice and dashed along the ledge. Below he heard a startled cry, and just as he rounded a shoulder of rock he heard the twang of a bowstring, immediately followed by the clatter of an arrow glancing off the granite not half a foot from his left ear. Kit reached the end of the ledge and, without breaking stride, or even considering the risk he was taking, he sat down and rode the sloping rock to the ground. It was the roughest, fastest slide he'd ever taken, with the coarse granite battering his tailbone every inch of the way. Kit felt sure he had worn a hole clear through the seat of his buckskin britches by the time he hit the ground hard and fast. He rolled once in the deep snow, sprang to his feet, and sprinted for the nearest horse.

An intervening tree caught the next arrow in its branches. Kit leaped atop the nearest Indian pony and, grabbing a fistful of mane, gave a shout and a kick, and was instantly plunging through the forest. He leaned low to avoid the lashing tree branches, using leg pressure to try to steer the galloping horse, for in his mad dash he had failed to grab its reins, and for the moment they dragged the ground, out of his reach. Kit had no idea at first in what direction he was riding, only that it was away from the Comanches, and that was good enough. But after a minute he noticed that the horse was following its own tracks back . . . back to the ravine and the dead dogs . . . back to the rest of the Comanches in the clearing where Kit had first caught sight of them!

Kit tried to stop the animal, tried to turn its head. But the horse had made up its mind to rejoin the others and there was no changing it. Kit had only one option now. He slid off the horse's back and tumbled to a stop against the trunk of a piñon pine. He lay there a moment as his body revisited all the places it ached, but no sooner had his head cleared than he heard the pounding of hooves coming up behind him. There wasn't a moment to waste licking his wounds. He scrambled to his feet and jogged away from the trail into the trees a heartbeat before the riders thundered past.

The Comanches did not see him, but his escape would not go undetected for very long. Kit paused only a moment to get his bearings, then cut through the forest, heading for the ravine. If he was lucky, he'd find his horse. He had no idea how far the ravine ran, or even if the animal had stopped fleeing, but Kit had to get back to warn Charlie Bent, and he could never outdistance the Comanches on foot.

With the Comanches not breathing down his neck, Kit again became aware of his body. His hand throbbed and hurt worse than the bullet wound he had taken in the shoulder a few years before from a Blackfoot warrior while helping his friend, Mark Head. His back muscles cried out with each jarring step. To look over his shoulder, Kit had to rotate his whole body. The neck muscles just weren't cooperating anymore.

"Helluva way to spend my birthday!" he grumbled to himself as he cut through the trees, trying to avoid sticks and rocks as best he could, considering the half a foot of snow covering the ground. He thought of Charlie and Hernando waiting for him miles ahead, and for an instant Kit wanted to get his fingers around the Mexican's scrawny throat for being the reason he was out here now, fighting half-wild dogs, dodging Comanche arrows, half-frozen, and hurting worse than a prairie dog in the middle of a buffalo stampede.

At least some good had come of it. He'd found Seth Wilson, and now the criminal would pay for his crime. The Colonel, Marjory Holmes's father, would certainly see to that, and so would Kit.

Kit drew up to catch his breath and check his bearings. The pounding blood in his ears nearly drowned out every other sound. Fat snowflakes continued to drift straight down from the windless sky. His breathing threw up a gray screen in front of his eyes.

Kit started moving again, this time at a brisk walk. He had just decided the ravine had to be nearby when all of a sudden the ground inclined sharply and Kit was standing at the very edge of it, several hundred yards above the place where he had nearly died at the jaws of the two dogs. The ravine continued on to his right, climbing as it cut back into the Sangre de Cristo Mountains. Kit did not see his horse anywhere around, but below, the tracks of a fleeing animal showed clearly in the snow. With any luck, the animal would have stopped on its own and would be waiting somewhere up ahead for him.

Then Kit heard the sound of their horses again. The Comanches had discovered his ruse and had doubled back. In this snow any fool could have followed his tracks—and the Comanches were no fools; they were superb trackers, even without nature's help. Kit scrambled down into the ravine and ran along his horse's tracks. A stunted piñon grew near the tracks. Kit jogged a few dozen paces past the tree, then very carefully walked backwards, placing his feet precisely in the prints he had already made.

At the piñon, he jumped clear of the tracks and hurriedly slipped behind the tree. Taking his rifle by the barrel in both hands, like a bat, he hitched it over his shoulder and waited.

The Comanches came to the edge of the ravine and halted. From his hiding place Kit watched them momentarily survey the deep gash in the land that lay before them. Then they started down into it, coming on cautiously, their bows ready, their eyes and ears alert for any sign of danger.

"Maybe he has run into some trouble, yes?" Hernando asked after another few minutes had passed without any sign of Kit.

Arms tightly folded against the cold, Charles Bent glanced at the Mexican and grimaced. "Kit can take care of himself," he said flatly. But he was worried about it too. Kit had been gone well over an hour, and the bone-penetrating cold didn't help to make the waiting any easier. "We'll give him some more time."

"Then what, *Señor* Bent?"

It was plain that if Bent went looking for Kit, both Hernando and Seth Wilson would be long gone by the time he returned. Bent said, "Then I'll tie you and that *hombre* to a tree and go looking for Kit."

"A tree!" Hernando exclaimed. "Sweet Mary, we will freeze to death if you do not come back for us!"

"Either that, or the wolves will get you," Bent agreed unemotionally.

"You are a hard man, *Señor* Bent."

"And you're a thief. Just be grateful I haven't hobbled you already." Bent strode a few feet along the trail, peered long and hard into the night, then came back, having reached a decision. "Fifteen minutes, Hernando. That's what I'll give Kit. Fifteen minutes, then you and me, and that *hombre* there will get moving again."

"Without *Señor* Carson?"

"Like Wilson said, Kit can trail a mountain goat up the side of Mr. Pike's mountain. He won't have any trouble following us."

"What if he is hurt?"

Bent was torn. Leave his friend and bring these two back to Taos, or go looking and risk losing Hernando and Wilson? What would Kit want him to do? Bent knew the answer to that. Kit would want Wilson and Hernando brought to justice. It was a hard choice, but Bent had waited long enough, and the time for hard choices had come.

"Kit can take care of himself," Bent repeated. "We'll give him another quarter hour, then we pull out."

Hernando shoved his hands deep into his pockets and turned away.

Wilson caught Hernando's attention with a quick jerk of his hand. Surprised by this, Hernando cast a glance back at Bent to see if he'd noticed. Bent hadn't. He had resumed his watch. Hernando turned a curious eye toward the wounded man.

Wilson gave another impatient wave.

In a casual manner, Hernando worked his way to the travois.

"You want out of here?" Wilson asked in a low voice when Hernando was near enough to hear.

"*Sí*, I would like to get away," Hernando acknowledged.

"You help me and I'll help you."

Hernando looked at him. "How could you help me?"

"I'm not as bad hurt as I'm making out. And I've got a . . ." He paused as if reconsidering. "I've got a plan as to how to take care of Bent, only I'll need your help. What do you say?"

Hernando didn't like what he heard in Wilson's voice. Wilson was not a man to be trusted, but on the other hand, Hernando was not eager to face Don Francisco Jaramillo, or the alcalde in Santa Fe, who was a stern government official with a heart of ice and a quick temper.

"Let me think about it."

"Sure, only not too long, Hernando. We've only got a few more hours to Taos. Once we reach it, our chance to get away will be gone."

"What about *Señor* Carson?"

"You just help me take care of Bent. If Broken Nose hasn't dealt with Carson, I'll finish him off myself. I've an old score to settle with that man and I don't intend to let it go unanswered this time."

Hernando was not sure about this. "What is it you would want me to do?"

"All you've got to do is help me get Bent over here and keep him distracted. I'll do the rest."

"How? You are bad hurt."

Wilson considered a moment, and after casting a glance at Bent, whose back was toward them as he peered out into the night, Wilson whispered, "Bent has a pistol under his coat. If I can get my hands on it . . ." He let his words trail off, leaving the rest of it to Hernando's imagination.

Hernando's eyes rounded. "You would kill him?"

"You want to go back and stand before the al-calde?"

"No . . . no I do not want that."

"I'll do what I have to. You in or out?"

Hernando frowned, and reluctantly he nodded his head. "*Sí*, I will help if I can."

Chapter Nine

Every muscle in Kit's body tensed as the two riders drew nearer. Then suddenly the Comanches stopped and peered hard at the trail that lay before them. Did they suspect the ploy, or had they caught a glimpse of him waiting for them behind the tree? Kit didn't see how they could have, with the night's deep shadows gathered close around the tree as they were. But then maybe, like Kit, these two had been alerted by that mysterious sixth sense which tends to make itself known fullest in men who live their lives beyond the safe borders of civilization.

The Comanches discussed the matter between them. Kit held his breath. After a moment one of the Indians nudged his horse forward, coming ahead cautiously while his partner waited.

Something *had* alerted them.

Now the first man would see where Kit's footprints had ended and he would know immediately what he had done. Kit had planned to let the first man pass safely and take out the second Indian as he rode past. Now all that had to change. Kit had to rethink fast.

As the Comanche drew abreast of the tree, Kit knew there'd be no waiting for the second man, who still remained behind, watching, his bow ready. Kit had wanted to avoid using a gun, but now he could see no other way. Quietly he unbuttoned his coat to put the pistols quickly within his reach.

The first Comanche rode past. Kit let him go. He'd be back soon enough. Easing farther into the shadows, Kit shifted his rifle and, with the trigger held full back to eliminate the sound of the sear snapping into place, drew back the hammer and set it to full cock.

Up ahead, the Comanche spotted the place where Kit had reversed on his own tracks. He drew rein and stared at the footprints in the snow, and instantly understood the trick he had played on them. Turning, he shouted a warning to his partner. They both eyed the tree and Kit flattened himself upon the snow as an arrow whistled over his head. He propped himself on his elbows, sighted, and pulled the trigger.

The boom of Kit's buffalo rifle filled the ravine with noise and smoke and flame, and the Comanche lurched off his horse, his arms flung back as the big bullet slammed him to the ground.

The second Indian was bearing down on Kit at a full gallop, a bloodcurdling war whoop filling the night where the blast of Kit's rifle had left off. Reaching under his coat, Kit yanked one of his pistols free, cocking it as he swung it around. He pulled the trigger and the cap snapped . . . and that was all.

Dropping the useless weapon, Kit grabbed for his second pistol. The Comanche launched an arrow, which skidded off a tree branch. The Indian leaped from his horse and in the faint moonlight Kit's eyes locked upon the steel blade that had appeared in the man's fist.

Kit pulled the pistol free, cocked it, fired, and immediately rolled to his left. The Indian crashed headlong into the snow, gave a low groan, and curled himself into a tight ball, cradling his stomach with his arms. Kit shoved the pistols back under his belt, grabbed his rifle from the snow, and catching the reins of one of the Indian ponies, swung atop it and kicked the animal into motion.

He came upon his own horse a few hundred yards farther on, at a place where dense growth clogged the gully and prevented any further travel. Quickly switching mounts, Kit urged his horse up the side of the ravine, pointed its nose south, and rode away from there as swiftly as he dared through the blanket of snow.

Broken Nose stood beside his horse in deep concentration, his dark eyes boring into the shadows as if they could somehow pierce through them.

Diego spoke to the Indian, but the war chief appeared not to hear him.

Louder, Diego said, "We will lose them if we wait too much longer, Broken Nose."

When the chief looked over, concern was heavy upon his scowling face. He considered Diego silently, then shifted his view to Long Runner and was about to speak when the distant boom of a rifle came from the forest.

At the sound, every head turned. The echo died away as they stood there staring off into the darkness. Silence swept back over them again, only to be shattered by a second shot—a sharper crack this time.

"A *pistola*," Diego said.

Broken Nose barked an order for his men to mount up. He instructed the herders to remain with the horses while the rest of them would go see what had happened. Long Runner rode in the lead, scouting the trail. It was a wide, well-trampled track by this time and it led first to the ravine.

Broken Nose leaped from his horse and knelt in the bloodied snow between the two dead dogs. He placed a hand upon them to feel for some remaining life. But Diego knew that all he felt was the eternal cold which had already begun to penetrate their bodies. When Broken Nose looked back at his warriors, it was with a new and more ardent fire burning in his dark eyes.

Diego was filled with delight at the sight of the dead dogs. How he had despised those beasts. How they had despised him! But just the same, he held back the wide smile that wanted out, guarding his true feelings. It would not be wise for Broken Nose to see his joy over the dogs' cold and lifeless forms.

Long Runner spied something and bent to study a moccasin print in the snow. He glanced up at his chief. "Look at this."

The chief left the dogs and hunkered down next to the scout. "What did you find?"

Diego listened closely, trying to understand their conversation with his limited Comanche. He missed some of it, but his ears perked up when he sorted out that the moccasin print was the same print Long Runner had discovered in the camp of the murdered *Comancheros*.

Ah, so now there is something more than just the rifles to make you want to find my brother's murderers. Good, good.

The loss of two dogs was nothing compared to the loss of a brother, but Broken Nose had cared for those half-wild animals as if they had been kin of his. He would not let the killing go unavenged, and that meant that surely Tomas's murderers would die before this day was over!

Mounting up, they followed the trail where it climbed the side of the ravine. A little way beyond, Long Runner reined to a stop again and slid to the ground. Here two sets of tracks crossed, one going south, the other heading west. But curiously, Long Runner told Broken Nose that the same moccasin made both tracks. They were somewhat trampled by the horses of the warriors sent on ahead.

Broken Nose ordered half his men to follow one set while he and Long Runner followed the second. Diego stuck with Broken Nose and soon they were standing at the edge of another ravine—or perhaps the same one—Diego couldn't be certain. But he was certain that the pony standing down there was one of the Comanches'. The two dark forms lying upon the snow didn't move.

Broken Nose's anger swelled as his men lifted the bodies of their dead comrades upon their horses—the second pony had been found a little way up the ravine by the warriors Broken Nose had sent to scour the area for any trace of the man responsible for this carnage.

Inwardly Diego smiled. *And yet two more reasons to see that Tomas's murderers are found!*

Just then the other Comanches returned. Slung across the withers of one of the horses, its rider sitting far back, was a third body.

No, three more reasons! Diego couldn't have been more pleased.

Broken Nose sent a rider back for the remaining men and the horses. A few minutes later the company of Comanches were all together again and they started on the trail of the one who had done this.

Riding hard, Kit came upon the tracks that their horses and the travois had left in the snow. The faint glow to the east told him that dawn was nearing. When he thought about the night just past, a weighty regret over the five men who had died so far pressed heavily upon him. If there had only been some other way . . . But in each case the dead men had not left him any other choice. Kill or be killed seemed to be the unchanging code of the mountains—still, it was a mighty unsatisfying way to spend one's birthday, and the day before Christmas. Kit abandoned that line of thinking. He had no time for rueful musings. He had to reach Bent and warn him of the Indians following them. He had no way of knowing how far behind him the Comanches were, but Kit was certain it would not be very long before they discovered the bodies he had left in his wake.

Kit hurt in more places than he could count, but

he kept up a steady pace, turning in the saddle every now and then to check his back trail. So far there was no sign of the Comanches, but that meant nothing.

They would be coming after him. It was only a question of when.

Charlie Bent spun about and his eyes narrowed suspiciously at Hernando and Wilson. "What are you two palavering about?" he demanded.

Hernando took a hasty step away from the travois and grinned. "Only the weather, *Señor*. I think it will be a good day. Look, the snow is stopping already, and there is the hint of dawn in the sky. Once the sun, she comes up, it will be much warmer. No?"

Wilson said, "If I manage to live that long."

"You'll live until then," Bent said.

Wilson coughed. "I think I'm still bleeding. You wouldn't just step over here and take another look? I can hardly move or I'd do it myself."

"I already done that. You stopped bleeding hours ago. I told you I didn't want to hear any more of it."

"It must have started up again. I'm feeling sorta like I might pass out."

"Good. Then I won't have to listen to your griping anymore."

Wilson glared at Hernando. The Mexican cleared his throat and said weakly, "*Señor* Bent, if he dies, *Señor* Carson will not be happy."

"He isn't going to die." Bent frowned, then snorting a cloud of steam in disgust, he relented. "All right, I'll take another look." He set his rifle aside and, throwing back the horse blanket, began to unbutton Wilson's coat.

Hernando took another step backwards.

Wilson moaned when Bent probed the place on his shirt where blood had already dried and crusted over. His hand went for the slit where Bent's coat gapped.

Hernando watched Wilson's fingers creep toward the pistol Bent kept there. Hernando's breath caught and his teeth kneaded his lower lip. Suddenly he rushed forward and stuck his head in the middle of Bent's examination. "Does it still bleed?" he asked anxiously, and in his curiosity he managed to step between Bent and Wilson and muscle Bent out of the way.

"Hernando! Do you mind?"

"I am sorry. I am so clumsy. I was only curious, *Señor*."

Bent pulled Wilson's coat shut. "No, it does not still bleed, Hernando." Shifting his view to the wounded man, he continued, "And I don't want to hear another peep out of you."

Wilson speared Hernando with a burning glare. Hernando backed away . . .

Just then the pounding of an approaching horse drew their attention. The opportunity had passed again, and the hateful glare that Wilson gave Hernando was like a fist reaching out and throttling him.

Hernando gave a silent sigh of relief just the same. Although he feared going back to face Jaramillo or the alcalde, he did not wish to see Charles Bent killed either.

Kit Carson sawed at the reins, bringing his horse to a halt.

"Where have you been all this time?" Bent groused. Then, seeing his friend step stiffly out of the saddle, he took a closer look. "What the blazes happened to you, Kit? What happened to your hand?"

Kit managed a wry grin. "I had me a tussle with a couple dogs. All in all, Charlie, it's been a busy night. They were back thar, just like I figured. Maybe eight or ten Comanches, a Mexican, and a dozen or more horses that I reckon they were fixing to trade for those rifles we took."

"Dogs?"

"I'll tell you all about it later. Thar's no time now."

"You look beat, Kit."

"I feel worse than I look. But I can't let that slow us down. I suspect in a short time we're going to have our hands filled with Comanches, and before that happens we'd better find us someplace to make a stand. Thar's no way we can make Taos ahead of 'em—not towing Wilson thar."

"How about we just leave them the rifles? That's what they're after."

Kit frowned. "That might have worked a couple hours ago, Charlie."

"What do you mean?"

"Besides them two dogs I mentioned, I left three dead Injuns. I don't think the Comanches are gonna settle for a couple of crates of rifles. Thar out for scalps now—mine in particular."

Bent shot a glance at Hernando. "You heard Kit, saddle up." Grabbing his rifle, Bent gathered the reins to both his horse and Wilson's.

Kit took a minute to quickly reload his guns. He swung stiffly back onto his mount. "You got any notions of a place to put our backs up against, Charlie?"

"I know of a canyon not far from here. It's got steep walls with lots of little caves all along them. Indians used to live there long ago, or so I hear tell. But they've been abandoned longer than anyone can remember."

"I know the place," Kit said, glancing over his shoulder. "Let's ride!"

Chapter Ten

Kit dropped back a hundred feet or so as had been his habit since leaving the *Comancheros'* camp. He was less likely to become distracted here, away from the others, and the muffled plodding of the horses ahead of him was far enough off that it would not cover other sounds—like those of approaching hoofbeats from behind. From here Kit could give Bent a warning shout and a head start if the Comanches should come up suddenly. If that were to happen, Kit considered cutting out to one side or the other, to split the Indians' ranks. But he rejected that notion. It would have left Bent to fight alone. Hernando could not be counted on, and Wilson would certainly do all he could to make matters worse for the ex-trapper turned businessman.

Bent swiveled in his saddle and called back, "The place is just ahead, Kit."

Kit nodded. He saw it too; narrow canyon walls looming dark against the white carpet that blanketed the rolling land. The piñon trees had thinned considerably. The riders were leaving the forest behind, entering a country more open, more rocky, with sage scattered among the short, high desert pines. The snow had finally stopped falling, and the moon had drifted out of sight, but dawn's rosy promise, faintly brightening the eastern half of the sky, was about to be fulfilled.

The snow took on a soft pink tinge as they headed through the narrows and down into the broad canyon. Bent followed a trail near to one wall, hugging the sandstone cliffs where hundreds of pit-like caves dotted its shadowy face, looking a little to Kit like the whole valley had once been infected with smallpox. Kit had passed through here a couple times in the past, and once he had even stopped to climb into a few of the caves. None was very large, but each seemed to have once been a home to someone. The ceilings were blacked with the soot of ancient fires, and in some of the caves bits and pieces of pottery still remained. Scratching around one of them with a stick, Kit had managed to uncover a woven basket buried in the accumulated dust, still filled with dried corn.

But now there was no one here. Just the empty holes and worn footpaths . . . and the ghosts of that long-vanished people. Kit was certain a few of those spirits could still be found if a person looked hard enough—which he had no intention of doing.

As they rode, Kit had a vaguely uncomfortable feeling about what they were planning to do. If he'd been sharper, if his hand had not hurt so bad and the pain had not clouded his thinking, he would have recognized what it was that had sounded the warning at the back of his brain.

Turning their horses into a field of boulders, shaped by wind and rain over thousands of years, they dismounted, hoisted Seth Wilson between them, and followed a path to the nearest cave. A piñon jay scolded them from its perch atop a stunted, twisted pine struggling for a foothold between a crack in the rock. The brightening dawn revealed the tracks of coyotes who had spent the night prowling through the caves searching for mice and kangaroo rats.

It was no warmer inside the cave than outside, but at least here no one could get at them except by a frontal approach. Something about that thought nagged at him, but Kit was cold, hungry, tired, and hurting, and his thinking was not particularly clear.

The cave was only ten or twelve feet deep. They set Wilson against the back wall. Kit went out to collect an armful of the dead wood which littered the area, and dumped it inside the cave. Bent went to work constructing a small fire while Kit moved their animals to a protective circle of rocks a few yards away, out of the line of fire, and tied them to a tree.

Back inside the cave, Kit glanced at Seth Wilson. Leaning against one of the smooth, curving walls, Wilson gave him a hateful glare in return. Kit knew what the man was thinking. Given half a chance, Wilson would have his revenge, even if it meant his own death. And Kit had the Comanches to worry about too. Fishing around inside his hunting bag, he found a rawhide thong and bound Wilson's wrists.

"What's this for?" Wilson demanded.

"When your Comanche friends come a-visiting, I don't want to be worrying about what's happening at my back."

"I'm all shot to pieces and about to cross over," Wilson returned. "What hurt can I do you now?"

Kit gave a short laugh. "I'd judge that you're about as helpless as a wounded white b'ar."

"You're a sonuvabitch, Carson!"

Grinning, Kit took up his rifle and stood. His head nearly brushed the cave's rounded ceiling. "I'll say one thing for you, Wilson, that bullet didn't sweeten you up none. You've got just as much vinegar in you as you did the last time we met."

"I should have killed you then."

"I seem to recollect that you and your partners tried."

Wilson scowled and gave a slight roll of his shoulder as if recalling that last meeting, and the bullet that Kit had put in him. Kit remembered the incident as if it had happened only a week before. It was up north of here about two hundred miles, near Pike's Peak. Kit had tracked Wilson and his partners to a grove of cottonwood trees along the Fontaine-que-bouille—Fountain Creek as some of the Americans were beginning to call it. He'd managed to rescue the girl that they had kidnapped, and to kill Wilson's companions. But Wilson had fled into the trees. Kit had grabbed one of the dead men's rifles and fired, but the rifle shot high and to the left, only wounding Wilson. By the time Kit had retraced his steps, Wilson had

Doug Hawkins

taken a horse and was long gone. Kit could have trailed him and finished the job, but he had the girl, Marjory Holmes, to think about. After all that she had been through, he knew the best thing was to get her back to her waiting father.

Thinking it over, Kit wondered if not going after Wilson had been a mistake. He looked back at the man huddled against the dark sandstone wall. Well, he had him now, and if he didn't get careless . . .

Bent said, "Do you think those Comanches will follow us here, Kit?" He had gotten a small blaze started and was feeding in sticks.

Kit mused that it might have been the first fire this cave had seen since its former occupants abandoned it years, maybe even centuries, before. "They'll be here." He peered out the mouth of the cave. The cliff faced east, and soon the morning sun would be warming it, but now darkness still clung to the valley floor. "I'm going to ride back a ways to keep an eye out for them, Charlie."

Bent looked at him and frowned. "You look as if you could use some rest. How's the hand?"

Kit flexed his fingers, feeling the tightness. He held his hands over the blaze, warming them. "Long as I keep using it, I'll be all right. Can't afford to rest just yet, Charlie. Keep an eye on those two while I'm gone."

"Just make sure you're back here before the shooting starts."

"I plan on it." Kit glanced at Hernando, who had bent near the fire to warm himself. "Do I have to tie you up too?"

"No, *Señor* Carson."

Bent said, "You know, Kit, if we had an extra rifle or two, Hernando might be of some help."

"You trust him?"

Bent looked at the Mexican and frowned thoughtfully. "Not with my gold. But I think he knows he stands a better chance with you and me than with the Comanches, don't you, Hernando?"

"My shooting, she is not so good, but I will help if I can."

Kit nodded briefly. "All right, I'll bring up extra rifles."

"And Wilson's powder and hunting bag. I left them on my saddle. They might come in handy."

Kit hurried to their horses, pried the lid off one of the crates with his butcher knife, and removed two guns. They were inexpensive trade rifles with unadorned locks and plain, straight-grain wood, but they appeared to be of good quality. Sticking his little finger into the barrel, Kit judged them to be about 32-bore—same as his buffalo rifle. Back inside the cave, he gave them and Wilson's hunting bag to Bent, who immediately loaded both of the rifles.

"I'll be back soon."

Kit ducked outside, swung up onto his horse, and turned its head back toward the mouth of the canyon. As he rode in the growing dawn, that soft warning voice sounded in his head again, but Kit couldn't quite make out what it was trying to say to him. Just before reaching the mouth of the canyon, he crossed a game trail that switchbacked up the face of the cliffs. He reined over and took it to the top. Morning's first sunlight was about to burst over the mountain peaks to the east by the time he reached the level ground above.

From here he could see the snow-covered countryside below and the forest that they had just come from. The brightening morning gave him a clear view of it all. When the Comanches did show up, Kit would know it.

He dismounted to wait, and tried not to think about the warm fire that would be burning in Don Francisco Jaramillo's hearth at this moment. A fire Kit could be sitting next to if Hernando had not pilfered Jaramillo's gold. He grimaced to himself and shooed the thought from his head. Living in the past was a fool's game, and one Kit seldom ever played. But today was different. Today was his birthday—and Christmas Eve day—and there were better ways to spend such notable occasions than trailing thieves and fighting Comanches.

The teeth wounds in his hand burned and hurt all the way to his shoulder. Kit tried putting it in the snow to quench the fire, but that only made his fingers stiffen up more. All he could do was ignore the pain and wait, and wonder what was taking the Comanches so long.

Broken Nose brought his band to a halt and leaned forward, peering hard at the narrow canyon walls ahead. He knew this place, the lodges of the dead, and he did not like it. Once past the narrows, a wide canyon opened; a canyon dotted with hundreds of small caves. The perfect place for a group of well-armed men to make a stand.

Broken Nose dismissed the narrows as a place for an ambush. His view played across the open land that lay before the high cliffs. Intuitively, he knew it would be there, or just past the narrows, where an ambush might happen. The narrows

110

were too obvious a place and even though he did not know the men he trailed, he understood them well enough to know that they would be too clever to stage an attack there. No, it was better to attack before the narrows, while most men's eyes would be focused ahead, scouring the cliffs, or after them, when their guard might be lowered.

Broken Nose grinned to himself. It was how he would do it.

Long Runner rode up alongside his chief. "If they are waiting for us, it will be on the other side."

"Yes, I agree. In the lodges of the dead ones."

"We could lose many men," the scout pointed out.

"There are only three, and the friend of Diego." Broken Nose looked long and bitterly at the ponies bearing the bodies of the warriors he had lost to the white man. Like Diego, the Comanche war chief now had strong reasons to want to see these white men dead and their scalps hanging from his lodge pole.

"Let me go ahead and see what lays beyond."

Broken Nose nodded. "It is wise to determine their position before riding into battle. Take special care, my brother. This white man is wise to the ways of making war. I will move the horses up near the canyon and wait for your return."

Long Runner rode off, keeping to the trees as he made a wide loop to the west then turned south toward the end of the valley. If the white men were waiting inside it, they would be looking to the north, expecting an attack from that direction.

Threading through the juniper and piñon, Long Runner entered the canyon at its far end. He reined to a halt and sat silently among the quickly melting shadows, his every sense alert. Slowly the thin, hard line of a smile cut into his weathered face. The white men were here. The slight breeze that curled through the canyon carried with it the odor of wood smoke.

They had built a fire to warm themselves.

Long Runner scanned the sandstone cliffs for telltale smoke. When he didn't see any he was not surprised. A small fire within one of the caves could easily hide smoke, but not the smell of it. Nudging his pony farther into the canyon, he paused a second time behind the shoulder of a rock, and dismounted.

The Comanche moved as silently as the smoke he was following. He jogged from tree to tree, from rock slide to outcropping. He covered several hundred yards in a few minutes, finally coming to a place where he could see up the length of the valley. Long Runner dropped to his haunches and crept the last few dozen feet along the cliff face until he reached a position where he could see the horses tethered together ahead. The morning sunlight glancing blindingly off the new-fallen snow shone upon the tawny sandstone cliffs, turning them the color of gold. There at the mouth of one of the caves something moved. Long Runner caught a glint of a rifle barrel as it pulled back into the shadows.

A small, satisfied grin touched the scout's lips. Just as he and Broken Nose had suspected, the white men were here, and they were waiting.

Long Runner eased away from there, made his way quickly to his horse, and turning it away, rode back to where Broken Nose and the others waited.

* * *

Kit shivered in the cold, trying not to think about it as his eyes narrowed searchingly. A few moments earlier his attention had suddenly been riveted. At first he wasn't certain what it was he had seen move down there—perhaps it was only a herd of elk . . . and perhaps not. But as the sunlight nibbled away at the shadows, he knew that it was not elk. It was a herd of horses among the trees. Kit spied the riders with them. They lingered there for a while, partly hidden, then slowly the men and animals emerged from their cover.

He watched the war party cautiously leave the forest's edge and ride toward the canyon's mouth. The Comanches were on their way.

Kit was about to swing back onto his horse to warn the others when suddenly the entire party came to a stop and just stood there. His curiosity piqued, Kit hunkered back down to wait and see what they were up to. Minutes passed. The sun climbed higher. Some of the Indians dismounted and blew steam into their fists. They seemed to be waiting for something to happen. Kit spied the Mexican among them, one of the *Comancheros*. A partner, no doubt, of Seth Wilson.

What was keeping them? Did the Comanches know there was an ambush waiting for them inside the canyon? Kit had little doubt the chief suspected it. If it was he down below leading these men, he would have sent someone ahead to scout out the canyon. The hairs at the nape of his neck began to tingle and suddenly he understood why they were waiting there. Quickly his eyes scanned the ground below. Nothing. Kit's view darted across the open land to where it merged with the forest they had crossed during the night. Although he saw nothing, Kit was certain now that the Comanches were waiting for a scout to return.

Mounting up, Kit hurried off the flats, down the switchback to the valley floor and back to the cave were Charles Bent waited for him.

"They know we're here, Charlie," Kit shouted as he reined to a halt. Sliding off the back of his horse, he tied it with the others and ducked into the cave.

"You seen them?"

"Thar waiting just beyond those narrows. My guess is they sent a man ahead to scout us out. Thar waiting for his return."

"I haven't seen anything move out on the canyon floor." Charles Bent pulled thoughtfully at his chin. "Well, we couldn't have outrun them before, and it's plain we can't now."

"I was hoping we could take them by surprise."

Bent grinned. "I was hoping to spend a pleasant day with Don Francisco, going over the company's books. And then I was looking forward to the fandango my new father-in-law has planned for tonight."

Both men glared accusingly at Hernando.

The Mexican gave a shrug of his narrow shoulders and a feeble smile. "I know, you think it is all my fault. No?"

"If you didn't go and steal Don Francisco's gold, none of us would be in this fix now. By the way, where did you hide it, Hernando?"

"I already got it, Kit. While you were away. The weasel had it on him all the time."

"He did?" Kit's burning glare returned to the Mexican.

"But it was not my fault, *Señor* Carson! I was forced to do it. My heart is held captive by the sweet *señorita* Maria Juanita Chacon. Her eyes, they shine like polished obsidian, her lips like bright cherries. Her smooth neck is soft, like a baby's touch, no? And her—"

"Hold it right thar, Hernando, you've worked your way far enough down that young lady's body," Kit said. "I've never met a man who can come up with more excuses than you."

"I for one am getting mighty tired of hearing about this *beautiful* creature," Bent put in. "Get your head out of the clouds, Hernando, and think about those Comanches on their way."

Hernando's face took on a worried look. "What if I should die here today? I would never see my wonderful Juanita again."

Seth Wilson gave a short, disgusted laugh. "I ain't never heard nobody carry on over a woman like you. The world is full of females for the taking. Why, if any woman ever demanded money of me, I'd set her straight." He raised his bound hands and formed a fist. "Women are good for only one thing, and I ain't about to start paying for it!"

"Enough out of you," Bent ordered. He glanced at Kit. "What a sorry lot we got mixed up with, heh?"

Kit gave him a wry smile and moved to the entrance of the cave, studying the narrows to the north. He turned an eye to the south end of the canyon, where it opened onto sage, short juniper, and scattered piñon pine which would remain all the way to Taos. The town wasn't far off now, but with Comanches on their tail, it might as well have been a hundred miles. Kit glanced across the valley to a lower line of sandstone cliffs still in deep shadows.

"At least it's warming up on this side," Kit noted.

"Probably why the early Indians picked these east-facing holes to live in," Charlie said.

"Probably," Kit agreed. "Got any of them little cigars left, Charlie?"

"I think I got a couple on me somewhere." Bent stuck a hand inside his coat, fished around a bit, and handed a slightly crushed cheroot to Kit. He drew a twig from the fire and put the flame to the tip of it. Kit drew on it, getting it to burn.

"Thanks." He squinted outside. The rising sun had begun to glare off the new-fallen snow. Once again he was aware of a nagging voice at the back of his brain, and this time he listened to what it was saying. All at once he understood why he had been so uncomfortable when they had picked this place to make a stand.

Kit recalled the thought he'd had when he'd first stepped inside the cave and looked the place over. It was a thought left unfinished; one that cried out for a reply. *Here no one could get at them except by a frontal approach . . .*

And suddenly Kit knew what that missing reply was. If no one could get at them except from a frontal approach, then just as truly, *they could not leave by any other way either*.

In their eagerness to find a defensible position, they had crowded into a cage with no back door!

Chapter Eleven

The sun climbed higher into the sky. Bent fed more wood into the fire. Wilson complained that Kit had tied his wrists too tightly. Hernando's smirk did not escape Kit's watchful eye. Wilson was getting back some of the suffering he'd put Hernando through.

The cave had warmed up enough so that their breath was no longer visible, but where Kit had stationed himself at its mouth, the air was chilly in spite of the sunshine.

"They're sure taking their sweet time of it," Bent said, squatting by the opening and peering out. "Where are they?"

Kit let his view slowly wander the length of the canyon. "Thar already here, Charlie." He kept his concern about getting out of the cave to himself for the moment. No need to burden Bent with that now. Kit reckoned that Bent would figure it out for himself soon enough.

"You've seen them?"

"I don't have to see Injuns to know thar nearby."

"Hmm?" Charles Bent stared at the narrows. "Well, I'd like to see them just the same."

"So would I. When I don't see Injuns, that's when I start to get worried."

"You worried now?"

Kit looked at him and grinned. "A mite more than I was thirty minutes ago."

Suddenly Bent pointed. "Over there, Kit."

The Comanches had begun to move the herd of horses through the narrows and into the canyon. As Kit and Bent watched, the Indians rounded the animals up and drove them into a small pocket in the side of the cliff.

"What do you make of that?" Bent asked.

It was plain enough what the Comanches were up to. They were making a show out of moving their animals to a protected place. Anyone really interested in protecting the horses would have kept them safely outside the canyon. There could be only one good reason for the maneuver now.

"Thar trying to distract us, Charlie. They don't yet know that we already know that they know we're dug in here."

Bent gave a shake of his head as he sorted out the meaning of Kit's tangled sentence.

Kit said, "Keep a sharp eye out. They'll be coming from the south, if I haven't missed my guess. Hernando!"

"Señor?"

"Take up a rifle. The Comanches are about to make thar move." Behind him, Kit was aware that

Seth Wilson had scooted along the cave's wall to a place out of the line of fire. Kit might not have liked the man, but at least Seth Wilson wasn't stupid. Kit said to Bent, "The bucks I ran into last night weren't carrying rifles."

"They'll have to get in close then," Bent observed.

"Once those Comanches lose a couple of men, they'll make new plans." Kit considered a moment. "So far that war chief has done everything I would have done. If it was me not able to get my boys close enough to root out an enemy, I'd sit back on my haunches and wait."

"Starve us out?"

"We'll give up for want of water long before we fail for lack of food, Charlie." Kit looked up at the sandstone that formed the mouth of the cave. The rock was heating up outside and melted snow had begun to drip. "We might want to save some of that," Kit suggested.

"Got a cup with my saddle." Bent stuck his head outside and looked around.

"Careful now, thar out thar," Kit said.

Not seeing any Indians yet, Bent scurried down to the horses, retrieved a cup from his saddlebags, and turned to start back.

Down among the brush that grew up along the bottom of the canyon, a Comanche suddenly stood and drew back his bow.

"Charlie! Get down!" Kit threw his rifle to his shoulder. Bent dove for the ground as the Comanche released his arrow. At that same instant, Kit squeezed off a shot.

The arrow skimmed past Bent's shoulder and buried itself into the ground. The Indian was not as lucky. Kit's bullet smashed him in the right shoulder, spinning him around and out of sight behind a clump of bushes. Bent scrambled to his feet and, ducking his head, made a dash for the cave. Kit swung a pistol and fired at movement down below. An arrow arched through the air from farther out in the canyon and glanced off the rock face inches from Kit's head.

Bent launched himself at the cave and dove the last dozen feet, rolling to a stop inside. "That was a close one," he said, eyes rounded.

"Too close," Kit agreed, pouring powder down the barrel of his rifle and chasing it with a patched ball.

Hernando crept timidly up to the opening and peered outside, his rifle ready. "I see no one, *Señor* Carson."

"You won't, not until thar ready to fire."

Bent extended a hand outside and pushed the tin cup under the dripping snowmelt. "Looks like we might be here a long time."

Kit flexed his fingers. He didn't have a long time. He didn't know how long he could keep using the hand before it stiffened up entirely. "We'll have to think of something soon, Charlie."

"Let me see that hand."

Kit grimaced. "Nothing you can do for it here." But just the same, he showed it to him.

"Those dogs done a real good job on you."

"It was only one dog."

"And that was one too many," Bent replied. "We need to get you some warm water and salts to soak it in. Ignacia makes a poultice that will help."

Kit glanced at Hernando, then back at Bent and

grinned. "Why don't we just have Juanita Chacon rub on it some?"

Bent laughed.

Hernando looked at them and gave a small smile. "It would be the touch of a goddess, no?"

Farther back in the cave Wilson groaned, "Oh, give me a break!"

An arrow whistled through the opening. The men rolled aside. Hernando shut his eyes and pulled the trigger of his rifle, sending a bullet glancing off a rock below them.

When they looked outside again, Bent said, "Reckon that rock won't be causing us any more trouble."

"Sorry, *Señor* Bent." Hernando looked embarrassed. "I am not very good with a rifle, no?"

Kit took the rifle and reloaded it. "I reckon not. You get back out of the way."

"Can I not help?"

"Think you can keep these rifles loaded for us?"

"*Sí*, that I can do."

Another arrow smacked harmlessly into the stone wall. Almost immediately following it, a voice called from outside.

"*Señor* Wilson, are you inside there?"

"Diego?" Wilson shuffled his way near the mouth of the cave. "Diego, is that you?"

"*Sí*. I am here with Broken Nose. He is very upset that he did not get his rifles."

"Tell Broken Nose to be careful where his warriors are putting those arrows."

"It is good to hear your voice, my friend. You hurt bad?"

"N—" Wilson caught himself. "Yeah, *amigo*, I'm shot up real bad here. They got me all tied up too."

"It will not be long before you are free."

Kit searched for the source of the voice, but Diego was keeping himself well hidden.

"Tell me, my friend, is the man who murdered Tomas in there too?"

"He is. He's a sonuvabitch named Kit Carson. I claim the bastard's scalp for my own! I've got a long-standing score to settle with him!"

"In good time, my friend. They are not going anywhere soon."

"There are only two of them, Diego," Wilson called back.

Kit had had enough, and he cocked his pistol, putting its muzzle against Wilson's forehead. "Another peep out of you and *your* scalp will be decorating the barrel of my rifle. You understand?"

Wilson glared at him, but he shut his mouth just the same and crawled back against the far wall of the cave.

"*Señor* Wilson?"

Kit called back, "No more talk. You want us, you'll have to come and get us." He pulled his head back inside the cave.

Bent grimaced. "Did you have to give them that invitation, Kit?"

"Reckon if I had asked them to pack up and go home they'd have done so?"

Both men flinched when a rifle shot rang out and a chunk of rock exploded from the back of the cave, showering them with stinging gravel.

"Reckon not," Bent admitted.

"Whal, now we know that someone down thar has a rifle." No sooner had Kit spoken than another bullet sprayed sand in their faces.

"Two rifles," Bent noted wryly.

The morning lengthened, and still nothing moved below on the canyon floor, except now and again when someone fired a shot or launched an arrow. The sun rose higher and warmed the cave. Kit broke up the fire, saving what wood was left for later, and hoping that between now and then he could figure a way out of this rat trap.

So far no one had made any attempt to take their horses. From his vantage point, Kit had a clear view of the animals. The Comanches knew that and had left them alone—for the time being.

After a while, Bent rested his head against the wall of the cave and closed his eyes. Kit wanted to do the same. It had been more than a day since either of them had had any sleep, and as the cave warmed up, fighting down the urge to close his eyes had become a real effort. But he couldn't afford to let down his guard now. Just the same, Kit let Bent catch up on some much needed sleep. When the next attack came, at least one of them would have gotten a little rest.

Kit noted that Hernando was nodding off too, but Wilson was wide awake and glaring at Kit.

"You gonna keep me tied up all day, Carson?" Wilson demanded when he caught the trapper's eye.

Hernando lifted his sleepy head and looked at both of them.

Kit said, "You're mighty feisty for a man who claims to be at death's door."

Wilson's eyes narrowed at the mountain man. The veins in his neck stood out like thick cords as the rage within him swelled. Unexpectedly, he shifted his scowl toward Hernando. He didn't say anything, just stared at the Mexican until he looked away.

Hernando said, "How long, *Señor* Carson, before the Comanches make their move?"

Kit shook his head. "I don't know." He returned his view to the bright valley floor. He wished he had an answer to that. But it was looking more and more as if his first notion had been correct; that lacking any easy way to root him and the others out of this cave, they would just sit back and wait until the cold or the need for water forced them out into the open.

Bent had begun to snore softly. Probably dreaming about ledger books and inventory, about wagon trains carrying trade goods west and returning east loaded down with beaver pelts and buffaloskins, Kit mused. The business world had moved in on the trapper's world, and when Charles Bent had been forced to make a choice, he'd chosen the former. Fighting Comanches was not his lot anymore. For the most part, Charles Bent and his younger brother William had formed a strong alliance with the tribes of the plains, each needing the other as the Indians became more and more dependent upon the manufactured goods that a few beaver pelts or a nice buffaloskin could buy them.

William Bent had worked especially hard to form close ties with the Arapahos and Cheyennes, and they respected him. Even the Comanches, who were always testing the Bents' right to the land, maintained an uneasy truce with the big adobe trading fort the brothers had built two hundred miles northeast of Taos, on the Territorial side of the Arkansas River.

Kit caught a glimpse of something moving below. He studied the place a long moment and his patience was rewarded by another small movement. It was no more than the twitching of a branch as might have been caused by the touch of a breeze wafting through the canyon. But there had been no wind just then. When another branch shook a few dozen feet farther on, Kit knew the Comanches were moving—and it was the horses they were moving toward!

Kit drew back the hammer of his rifle and forced his stiff finger to curl around the trigger. Sighting down the long barrel, he calculated the line of travel the unseen Comanche was taking and placed his sight upon a patch of ground barely visible beyond the stiff, stubby growth. Catching his breath, Kit steadied the rifle and waited.

A glimpse of a buckskin sleeve and the dark brown skin of a man's hand flashed briefly into view. Kit shifted his aim back about eighteen inches and pulled the trigger. The boom of the rifle shattered the silence of the canyon. Charles Bent lurched suddenly awake, looking vaguely confused. Down below, an Indian tumbled into plain view and rolled to a stop against a rock.

Bent instantly shook off his drowsiness and poked an eye around the edge of the cave, searching the glaringly bright landscape. "Did you get him?"

Kit nodded. "One of them Comanches was trying for our horses, Charlie," he said, passing his rifle to Hernando, who began at once to reload the piece as Kit took up one of the spares.

"That's just wonderful," Bent said bitterly. "Not only are we trapped here, but in short order those

Indians are going to get our animals, and then even if we do figure a way out, we'll be afoot."

"Reckon holing up in these caves was not the smartest move we ever made."

Bent mirrored Kit's grim expression. "Maybe it wasn't, Kit. At least in the open we might have outrun them . . . that is if we had shed ourselves of that Wilson fellow."

"Whal, there's no sopping up the milk once the cow kicks over the pail, I reckon," Kit said as his keen eyes probed the ground below for more movement. What Bent had said was true, but short of killing Wilson in cold blood, Kit could see no other way to have handled the situation. He would never have let Wilson go, and it was not in Kit's nature to kill the man, even if killing was what the scoundrel deserved.

The heavy report of a rifle boomed below. The two men flinched as a bullet gouged a chunk of sandstone from the wall. As the sound of it died away, a man's voice called up to them in Spanish.

"Killer of dogs and men, hear my words! I will let the two men with you go unharmed if you come out, and bring the one with you called Wilson."

Bent gave Kit a quizzical look. "Killer of dogs?"

Wilson piped up, "That's Broken Nose. It was his dogs that Carson killed."

Bent glanced at Kit. "Chief Broken Nose. I've traded with him some. What do you make of his offer?"

Kit grimaced. "Whal, it would save your and Hernando's hides."

"At the cost of your scalp," Bent pointed out.

Hernando handed Kit his loaded rifle back.

"Don't do it, *Señor* Carson. I have heard many horrible stories of what the Comanches do to their enemies."

Both men looked at the skinny Mexican with surprise.

Kit said, "It might be your only way out, Hernando."

"*Sí*," he said flatly, and Kit wondered if Hernando was suddenly reconsidering his rash remark.

Kit shifted his view to Bent. The businessman read the question that was in Kit's eyes and said, "Hell, you know what I think about it, Kit. You don't have to ask. Anyway, I never met a Comanche yet who could be trusted to keep his word. All they're trying to do is root us out of here."

"Don't listen to him, Carson," Wilson growled. "I'll see to it that Broken Nose makes quick work of you, and that he lets your friends go. Anyway, I wouldn't let them hurt the Mexican. He's as much a prisoner in all this as I am. Ain't that right, Hernando?"

Hernando made a point of not looking Wilson in the eye when he answered. "I would not want to see anyone die because of me, and what I have done," he replied meekly, eyes still averted.

Bent called back, "We don't like the terms of your deal, Mr. Broken Nose. But perhaps you'll consider ours. You and your boys pack it on out of here and let us go on our way unharmed, and we'll stop killing off your warriors. Seems to me that by now you're running short of men—especially since they keep poking their heads out and getting shot."

This time it was Diego who answered. "Not until

we get the man who killed my brother."

"Brother?" Bent looked at Kit, then both men looked back at Wilson.

"Tomas, one of the men Carson killed, was Diego's brother," Wilson said.

Kit gave a shake of his head and said, "Whal, now we know which way the stick floats with that one."

Bent agreed. "Where there's been family blood spilled, the fire of revenge burns mighty hot."

They returned their attention to the bright morning and the canyon's floor. It was almost noon now and a steady stream of snowmelt trickled down the rockface outside their cave, forming a rivulet that flowed along the trail toward their horses below. Another hour passed. Now and again a rifle would fire from below and spray the inside of the cave with stinging bits of sand.

Hernando remained against the back of the cave and to the right of the cave's mouth, safely out of the line of fire. As he sat there in deep, quiet contemplation, a drop of water fell from the dark roof of the cave and smacked him on the bridge of his nose. He wiped it off and shifted his view to the bright slash in the rock where Kit and Bent kept a watch outside.

It wasn't his fault they were in this fix. All he had wanted to do was impress that tightfisted Juan de Dios Chacon with the jingle of a little gold, in the hopes he would allow him to wed his lovely daughter.

It just wasn't his fault!

Another drop splattered against the collar of his coat. Annoyed, he shifted his position a few inches.

Plop . . . plop . . . plop . . . A big wet spot spread across the sleeve of his coat. Hernando looked at it, frowned, and moved a few more inches.

Would not another man in his shoes have done the same, he wondered? What mortal man could resist those lovely round eyes, those lips the color of rose petals? Where matters of the heart are concerned, perhaps the head does go to sleep—at least for a little while. But now Hernando was beginning to wake up to the results of his rashness. He pondered briefly if maybe there might not have been another way.

If only I could go back and do it over again!

But of course no one could do that. It appeared that only through death's doorway would he and the others make their way out of this doomed hole. *If there was only some way*, he argued with God, crossing himself, *I would never steal again—*

Ker-plop!

Hernando stared at the pile of snow suddenly in his lap. Slowly his head craned back and his view traveled up to the black roof arching overhead. A smaller icy glob splattered upon his forehead.

Hernando blinked, wiped his forehead dry, and squinted at the ceiling, trying to pierce the darkness above.

"*Señor* Carson?"

The sound of something heavy suddenly shifting positions came ominously from above him.

"*Señor* Carson?" he repeated, a little louder this time.

"What is it?" Kit answered abruptly, his eyes still focused outside.

"I think there is something happening here."

"What are you talking about?" Kit cast an impatient glance at the skinny Mexican.

Hernando was urgently poking a finger at the ceiling.

Bent looked over too.

Kit frowned. "What's gotten into you, Hernando?"

Plop. Wet snow splattered upon his face again. "Something is moving up there . . ." Hernando's voice trailed off in a warble and his eyes suddenly went wide as he leaped to his feet.

But it was too late to escape the huge snowslide that rumbled down from above, burying the Mexican.

Chapter Twelve

Kit and Bent each grabbed hold of a flailing arm and dragged Hernando from under the pile. The snow was heavy and wet, and Hernando emerged from it shivering and sputtering. Between sputters, Hernando cursed the snow and the cold and shook himself like a soaked dog. He shook a fist at the narrow slice of daylight that the snowslide had revealed in the ceiling of the cave.

"Why do these things always happen to me?" he moaned.

"You all right?" Kit asked.

"*Sí*, but I am very cold and very angry! What happened?"

Charles Bent peered up the long chute, studying it. "Looks like there's a fissure here that filled with snow during the storm. It's a natural chimney of sorts."

Kit's view traveled up the narrow, twisting fissure.

Bent continued, "The heat from our fire must have loosened it up."

"And the sun warming the rocks outside," Kit added, stepping around the pile of snow on the floor to take a look at it from a different angle. "It's at least thirty feet to the top."

Bent nodded, then suddenly realized what Kit was thinking. "You reckon a man could climb that thing?"

"If he could, it would take him to the top of this plateau."

"That would make for a better position to shoot from," Bent said.

Kit glanced at him. "Or other things."

"What do you have in mind?"

Kit studied the cleft for a moment without speaking. When he did, he said, "If a man could somehow make his way out of here unseen and manage to stampede those Comanche ponies, whal, that would give them Injuns something other than us to think about, wouldn't you say?"

Bent wasn't sure. "Would it, Kit? Would those Comanches break off their stakeout so easily?"

"At the very least, they'd have to send some men after them, and that would whittle down the odds some. Thar can't be but half a dozen left out thar anymore. Thar was less than a dozen when I first seen 'em, and since then five have gone to thar maker."

"Anything is better than staying here pinned down like we are," Bent said.

Kit said, "Hernando, keep an eye outside. Charlie, can you give me a boost?"

Bent locked his fingers and Kit put a moccasin into them. With a grunt, Bent heaved Kit up. Kit reached as far as he could, grabbed for a rock ledge at the tips of his fingers, and caught hold of it. But as soon as he tried to put his weight onto it, his right hand gave out and he slid back down.

Kit flexed his stiff fingers and winced at the pain. "Thar isn't any strength left in it," he said.

"Let me give it a try."

Kit eyed the heftier man. Although nearly the same height, Charles Bent had a good thirty-pound advantage over Kit. "You'll get yourself stuck, Charlie."

"Just give me a hand up."

Kit lent a leg, and steadying his friend with his left hand, helped Bent up into the fissure. Charlie found a finger hold and pulled himself up. Wiggling and twisting, he inched toward the jagged slash of light above. His feet receded up into the dark crevice as bits of rock clattered down out of the natural chimney. Then he stopped. Kicking and thrashing, clawing and pulling, Bent had reached as far as he could, and could not advance another inch.

"I'm stuck, Kit," he called down, and with a sudden raining of stones, Charles Bent came rattling out of the cleft and fell into the pile of snow.

"Almost made it, Kit," he said, shaking his head. "If I was only a couple inches thinner . . ." A thought suddenly occurred to him and he shed his heavy coat, tossing it to the floor, near Wilson's feet. "Let me give it another try."

Over by the cave's mouth, Hernando divided his time between looking for the Comanches and watching Kit help his friend back up into the cleft in the ceiling. Once again Charles Bent wiggled and squirmed, kicking and cussing and clawing his way up into the crack. His feet disappeared again. Kit craned his neck back, watching his friend's slow progress.

Out of the corner of his eye, Hernando caught a movement at the back of the cave. Wilson was reaching inside Bent's discarded coat. Wilson glared up at him, and the warning look alone was enough to silence the Mexican. In an instant Wilson had the businessman's pistol in hand, and in the next, he had it stuffed safely away in his own deep pocket. Wilson's burning look told Hernando that if he knew what was good for him, he'd keep his mouth shut.

Hernando gulped and quickly looked back outside. He didn't want to face Don Francisco for the theft of the gold, yet he didn't trust Wilson's offer to help him escape either. If he warned Kit now, Hernando feared that Wilson would surely kill the mountain man . . . or perhaps even himself! Wilson had only one shot available to him. Surely, Hernando reasoned, he'd try for Carson first.

In spite of the cold, Hernando was suddenly sweating. Because of him, men had already died, and more were likely to. If there was only some way to set it all right again—but he could never go back. What was done was done, and whatever the consequences, however it panned out in the end, the responsibility for what had happened would rest squarely upon his shoulders.

Oh, Juanita, for you I have risked everything. If only you cared as much for me as I for you, then money would make no difference. Gold could never stand between us no matter how much your father protested! For the first time Hernando allowed the truth to encroach upon his dreams. Although this was indeed an affair of the heart, if he was to be perfectly honest with himself, he would have to admit that it was an affair mainly of *his* heart. And now, for the hope of winning the woman's hand, he had caused so many deaths, and the killing, he knew, was not over.

But what could he do about it?

Hernando heard Bent curse the narrow gap, and the next moment, the burly ex–mountain man was clambering back out of it.

"I just can't make it, Kit," Bent said. "I'm too big in the chest, and getting that way in the rear end."

"It's all that easy living, Charlie," Kit replied with a note of resignation in his voice. Kit peered up again and shook his head. "I'm skinny enough to get through it if only . . ." he looked at his hand and frowned.

Hernando could see that Kit's hand had swollen to almost twice its normal size.

With a resolute set to his jaw, Kit said, "Give me a boost up, Charlie. I'll give it another shot."

"*Señor* Carson." Hernando was startled by the sound of his own voice, and even more startled by what he knew would come next. "I am skinny, no? Let me try it."

"You?" Kit looked from the Mexican to Bent. The businessman was just as surprised. "I don't know, Hernando. What could you do even if you did make it?"

"I can do whatever it is you need me to do," he replied confidently, although confidence was the last thing he was feeling at the moment.

Bent said, "How do we know you won't hightail it away from here just to save your thieving hide?"

"*Señor* Bent, I know you think so. I have not been honest in the past, it is true. And because of that, you both may die. Others already have. Please, let me do this one thing to help."

"I don't know," Bent growled.

Kit considered a moment. "You think you could make your way to where the Comanches have corralled thar horses?"

"*Sí*, I think I can."

"And stampede them, running them down the middle of that canyon and though the Comanches?"

"Stampede the horses?" Hernando grinned. "All my life I have tried not to do such a thing. But I have run down a stampeding herd a time or two, when I worked for *Señor* Saavadra. I can try," he replied honestly.

"You might get shot, Hernando. Might even get yourself killed."

He looked around the little prison they had backed themselves into, swallowed down a lump in his throat, and said, "The same, it can happen here, no?"

"You aren't going to trust him, Kit, are you?"

Kit tried to flex the fingers of his hand, then turned his eyes back up the narrow passage to the slit of blue sky far above them. "Reckon we don't have much choice in the matter right now, Charlie, unless you have a better idea."

He didn't. Ruefully, Charles Bent shook his head. "With your bad hand and my big rear end, I don't see any other way."

Kit drew a pistol from his belt and handed it to Hernando. "Know how to use this?"

Hernando looked at it, not taking it from Kit right away. "*Sí*, I have shot a gun before. My aim, it is not too good."

"So I recollect," Kit replied dryly. "But don't fret about that. You don't have to hit anything in particular, and I know you're good at that."

Hernando frowned.

Kit grinned at him. "All you need to do is get those horses running, and a shot fired behind that herd should do the job."

"Then what?"

"Then you wait for them Comanches to come and get you," said Wilson. "And when they do, they'll gut you like a mangy coyote and hang your scalp from a war lance."

"Charlie, why don't you stuff a rag between that crittur's choppers?"

Bent grabbed up his rifle and turned its muzzle toward Wilson. "I understand how it is, how Kit would like to get you back to the States in one piece, but another word out of you, mister, and this bullthrower of mine will finish the job that Kit's bullet started."

Wilson clamed up, giving Hernando a warning look as he turned away. Its message was plain enough. It said "keep your mouth shut or else." Hernando didn't like that "or else" part, and his already overstretched imagination colored in all the unpleasant possibilities. He already had the Comanches to fear; he didn't need to pile on any more worries, so he said nothing about the pistol Wilson had taken from Bent's coat pocket. Hernando took the gun Kit held out to him and pushed it through his belt, under his coat.

Kit said, "I'm afraid what he says is mostly true, Hernando. You don't want the Comanches to get thar hands on you."

"What should I do, *Señor* Carson?"

"Whal, if it was me, I'd try to hitch a ride on the back of one of them stampeding stallions. I'd grab me a hank of mane and lay low, and pray mighty hard that I'd make it past thar guns and arrows."

"Praying, *Señor*, is something I have been doing much of lately."

Kit grinned. "Sometimes we can't get enough of it."

Charles Bent made another stirrup of locked fingers, and as Hernando slipped a foot into it, Kit handed the Mexican his second pistol.

"You might need this one too."

Hernando considered the weapon a moment. He glanced at Wilson, then back at Kit; a dark, concerned look shadowed his face. "No, *Señor* Carson, I think you might need it more here than I will up there." He cast another quick look at the bound man, then quickly turned and stepped into Bent's waiting hands.

Bent easily hoisted Hernando into the fissure. The Mexican grabbed hold of a ledge and pulled himself up. Bracing elbows and legs against the narrow sides, he shifted his hands and reached higher for the next finger hold. Up he climbed, working his way slowly through the crack in the rock. In places, the cold sandstone squeezed in on him like a vise, crushing the air from his lungs. But each time, by pulling hard, Hernando managed to drag himself past the obstacle. Upward he strove, making slow progress through the torturous passage. Then his hand groped in the cold air, grabbed the edge of a rock, and the next instant Hernando was peering at the green needles of a scraggly piñon pine struggling for a foothold in the rocky soil.

Hernando heaved himself from the hole and lay flat upon the snow-covered ground, his eyes darting left and right, searching for the Comanches that he feared might have already discovered him. Nothing moved. The cold worked its way through his coat, making him shiver. Cautiously he elbowed through the snow toward an outcropping. Once behind it and out of sight from the canyon below, he let out a long breath.

Before him was scattered piñon and juniper stretching away upon the slanting land. Farther off was the forest they had crossed that night. He was beyond the canyon, beyond sight of the Comanches, and at the moment nothing lay between him and that forest . . . and *freedom*!

His fist reached beneath his coat and curled around the butt of the pistol there. A wave of excitement tingled through his body as he realized he'd been given a new chance at life. He seized the opportunity at once and started off in a crouch. By evening he would be at La Madera, he'd be with Juanita, and there would be no one to follow him!

All at once his excitement was swept away and a deep, brooding heaviness settled in its place. It was an obnoxious thing, unwanted, just squatting there in the middle of his breast, looking at him with grave, piercing eyes. No, not looking *at* him, he realized, but *through* him! Studying something—and that something, Hernando suddenly understood, was a little, dried-up growth barely alive within him called *character*. Startled, Hernando stopped and hunkered down behind a juniper to think this over.

What was he doing?

Hernando's view shifted between the forest and freedom on the one hand, and the canyon and perhaps death on the other. And even if he did survive the Comanches, there was still Don Francisco Jaramillo to face!

He was torn as he hovered there on the cutting edge of two choices.

"Think we made a mistake, Kit?" Charles Bent asked after Hernando had vanished up the crack and only blue sky filled the top of the long fissure. "Think he might just take his good luck on being such a skinny varmint to up and vamoose on us?"

Kit returned to his station at the mouth of the cave, holding his rifle in his left hand while slowly working the stiff fingers of his right. The sun-glare off the snow stung his eyes; it was impossible to look at for very long. But at least it contrasted sharply with the dark buffalo robes the Comanches wore to keep warm. Kit blinked and looked back into the shadows where Bent had remained, peering up the crack.

He couldn't know if they had made a mistake or not. He could only hope that somewhere inside the thief there remained a shred of integrity. "If we did make a mistake," Kit said finally, "are we any worse off for it?"

Bent frowned and shook his head. "I reckon not—except for the loss of a pistol."

"How well do you know Hernando?"

Bent thought it over a moment. "He's been Don Francisco's groom for about three years. He has always seemed a dependable fellow. Not one I would have thought would steal his *patrón's* money and run. But other than the few times I've met him at the Jaramillo homestead, I reckon I don't know him very well at all."

"Neither do I. I met him once when he worked on Pedro Saavadra's rancho. I was riding with Ewing Young at the time. Young had bought a remuda from Saavadra for a trapping trip we were planning to make into Mexico. Hernando was one of the vaqueros who had brought the herd of horses in. He was a mite on the tender side back then, but he handled those horses like the best of the older vaqueros, like he was born to the saddle. He rode as good as any man there, and I won't say that he couldn't ride a circle or two around me."

"Hernando is good with horses," Bent agreed. "That's why Jaramillo hired him." Bent paused, pushing out his lower lip in a thoughtful manner. "Just what are you getting at, Kit?"

"If we did make a mistake, we've lost only the pistol, but if we didn't, I can't think of anyone here better able to stampede those horses and yet keep enough control over them to make them run where he wanted them to."

Wilson laughed and said, "You're dreaming, Carson. That Mexican will be long gone by the time Broken Nose lifts your scalp. I know his kind. The greaser's on his way out of here even now. He's got his own skin to worry about. Hey, how about untying my hands now?"

Kit looked at the bound man a moment, then at Bent. "Charlie, when we get back to Taos, remind me to brush up on my pistol shooting."

"Why's that?"

"Because the next time I have the good fortune to put a bullet in that worthless polecat, I want it to take."

Bent grinned as he shrugged back into his heavy coat. "I saw a couple of old whiskey jugs out behind Don Francisco's house. I'd judge them to be just about the size of a man's head—*his* head," he added, hooking a thumb over his shoulder at Wilson. "I'll set them up on the wall when we get back. I'll even paint eyes on 'em for you if you want me to."

Chapter Thirteen

"*Señor* Wilson?"

At the back of the cave, Seth Wilson straightened up out of his slouch. "I am glad to hear your voice, *amigo*. How is it going in there for you, heh?"

Kit swung his buffalo rifle. "One word to them about Hernando and it will be your last."

Wilson snarled defiantly at Kit and said in a low voice, "What about taking me back to the States to stand trial?"

"I've been giving that some thought, Wilson, and I've about decided that it doesn't really matter one way or the other anymore. The fact is, it'd be a whole lot easier on me if I planted you right here. All I'm looking for is an excuse."

A long, tense moment passed as Wilson stared at the barrel of Kit's rifle. Then a small grin emerged upon his face, followed by a short laugh.

He looked out of the cave and raised his voice. "I'm doing just dandy, waiting for you to get me out of here, Diego. It's mighty cold and my belly is starting to complain."

"Enough said," Kit ordered sharply.

Bent moved up to the opening and peeked around it. "See them yet?" he whispered.

"No. They're taking particular care to keep out of sight."

"Learn quick, don't they? Wonder how Hernando is doing?"

Kit shook his head. "Least we know one thing."

"What's that?"

"The Comanches haven't got him."

"How can you be sure?"

"They'd let us know about it if they had. And if he was still alive, maybe even try to use him as bait to root us out of here."

Bent lowered his voice. "You don't believe what Wilson said about Hernando running out on us, do you?"

Kit grimaced. The question in Kit's mind was whether a polecat like Hernando could ever really change his stripes. "For your sake and mine, I hope he's wrong."

"*Señor* Carson?"

Kit looked back out into the glare but saw nothing. "What the hell does he want now?"

Bent grinned. "You can bet it's not a social call."

Kit raised his voice. "What is it, Diego?"

"It is getting late in the day, and it is very cold, no?"

"I haven't noticed."

"Maybe we can talk, make a deal? It is Christmas Eve. I do not want to spend it here with these savages. My woman and children, they wait for me to come home. There will be a Mass tonight at the church, and my wife, she will want me to go with her."

"Reckon she's just going to have to go by herself," Kit shot back.

"That would make her very unhappy. And when she is unhappy, my humble house, it can be a very uncomfortable place to live, *Señor*."

"Go on home to your wife and young'uns, Diego. No one is keeping you here."

"But you have my friend in there with you. You must release him. Then we can *all* go home."

Bent looked at Kit. "Is that *hombre* on the level?"

"You heard what Wilson said. One of those men I killed back at thar camp was his brother. What do you think, Charlie?"

"Hmm. I think he's hoping we'll lower our guard long enough for him and his Comanche friends to make a charge."

"That's about how I see it."

"Do we talk, *Señor* Carson?"

Kit put his rifle to his shoulder and slanted an eye along its barrel. "All right, Diego. Why don't you come up here and we'll powwow awhile?"

From a hidden position down below, Kit heard Diego's short laugh. No, *Señor*, you come down here. No one will shoot you. I give you my word."

"In that case, I'm afraid you'll be missing church tonight, Diego."

Someone fired at the cave. Kit squeezed off a shot at the puff of smoke that rose from behind a clump of bushes. Then once again the canyon fell eerily silent. They were out there just waiting, slowly shifting positions and working their way closer. Backed into this cave as he was, there was nothing Kit could do to stop it. Soon they would be close enough to rush the cave, and when they did, the fighting would become hand-to-hand in short order.

Kit frowned at his swollen hand, trying his fingers again. The hand would be useless in that sort of fighting.

Hernando, he thought, pulling back into the shadows of the cave to reload his rifle, *where the devil are you?*

"What are you doing? Have you gone loco in the head?" Hernando scolded himself as he crawled across the snow-covered ground, keeping to the rocks and the scant growth that peppered the mesa's top. "You will get yourself killed!" he warned himself. "You will never hold Juanita in your arms, never feel the warmth of her lips, never know her love, if you do something foolish now!"

He stopped behind a low boulder, where the sun shone bright but did little to warm the air, which was so cold it seemed to snap in his ears, as if somehow just moving through it shattered all the tiny ice crystals that sparked before his eyes when the sunlight was just so.

Hernando was still torn. He had been given an open doorway to freedom, and yet, for some unfathomable reason, he had chosen to remain here to help Kit and Bent.

What am I thinking?

These men were bound and determined to take him back to Taos to face up to his crime! They were his friends ... of sorts, but not close friends—certainly not close enough to risk his life for!

Again he cursed himself. He was not a warrior. He wanted only peace for himself and to be with the woman he loved. A sudden despair pressed down on him. If only Juanita felt the same passion toward him as he toward her. Quickly he shooed that thought from his brain.

Moving in a crouch, Hernando scurried to the next bit of cover, looking in every direction as he moved, terrified that a Comanche would pounce upon him. His fist tightened around the pistol, but he wasn't certain if, given the chance, he would even be able to use the weapon to defend himself. He was not a fighter, he was a lover! . . . and he was not even very good at that, he was forced to admit to himself. Had Juanita ever been more than just courteous to him? Had she ever really encouraged his affections? Two days ago he would have insisted that she had. But much had happened since he'd spied Don Francisco Jaramillo setting the pouch of gold coins upon his dressing table, and the next instant, when impulsiveness had overridden common sense, and he'd stolen that pouch.

He had been a fool. If only he had been content to remain Don Francisco's groom, tending the horses, all would be different now. He would have a warm fire to sit near, food to eat, friends to chat with, and no Indians to worry about. Horses were the only thing Hernando truly understood.

Hernando paused to look around and get his bearings. He was more confused now than ever. In all his darting and crawling through the snow, he worried that he had gotten turned around. Was he still going the right way? Might he be creeping right into the arms of the Comanches even now?

All Hernando could do was press on. To his great relief no Comanche leaped from behind bushes or rocks. Then a noise brought him to a stop.

It was the low whinny of a horse—followed by another.

He hardly breathed, listening, his eyes shifting nervously back and forth. He heard it again and knew at once that he was headed in the right direction. The sounds came from his right, and not very far away. Hernando let go of a long breath. He hadn't gotten turned around after all! Swallowing hard, Hernando quietly moved toward the sound. The dry snow squeaked beneath his boots, sounding louder to him than it actually was.

The ground suddenly fell away before him. Hernando wormed his way to the edge of the ravine and hid behind some rocks. Below him was the small box canyon where the Comanches had herded all their horses. Some of the animals wore blankets and the flimsy saddles that the Comanches sometimes used. Most were not saddled. Five carried the bodies of men. Three of these bodies were Indians. Hernando recognized the two men that Kit had left behind at the *Comancheros'* camp: Tomas and Pedro. One of the horses wore a Mexican saddle with a huge pommel. That would be Diego's horse, Hernando decided. In all, he counted nearly thirty animals in the box canyon.

There had to be a someone watching over the horses. After some searching, Hernando spied an Indian at the mouth of the side canyon, huddled inside a buffalo robe. The Comanche's attention was turned outward, toward the floor of the main canyon. He didn't appear to have a rifle, yet there was no way to know what weapons the Indian might be clutching beneath the robe. But one thing was obvious to Hernando, the Indians weren't expecting an attack on the horses. At least he had surprise on his side, and that bolstered him some.

Hernando drew in a breath, held it a moment, then let it out. He knew what had to be done, and he was stalling now. The longer he delayed, the greater was the risk that another Comanche might show up, or that the Indians in the canyon would overpower Kit and Charles Bent, and that would surely mean that he would be next, for the Comanches were excellent trackers. He had no choice but to go ahead with this crazy plan and pray to God he didn't lose his life!

Quickly Hernando crossed himself, and with a plea for mercy to the Blessed Virgin upon his lips, he started down into the canyon. In a minute he had made it to the bottom and was slowly creeping among the horses, whispering soft, soothing sounds, running a hand along their flanks in a calming way. Horses, Hernando mused as he eased toward the one wearing the saddle, were his gift. He had been a fool to forsake that for a pouch of gold and the hopes of winning the hand of a woman through the approval of her father.

If he ever got out of this alive, he would— Just then a rifle shot riveted his attention. He looked to the mouth of the box canyon, where the guard had come suddenly alert. A moment later a second rifle boomed. Hernando recognized the sound of it. He had heard that big gun boom once before in the camp of the *Comancheros*. It was Kit Carson's buffalo rifle.

Something was happening out in the canyon, and Hernando knew that Kit and Charlie needed his help!

"Over there!" Bent barked, pointing. He threw his rifle to his shoulder, drew a bead, and fired.

"Did you get the crittur?" Kit asked, sidling up against the mouth of the cave and peering out.

"Don't know for sure. But I don't think so, Kit."

"Thar getting a mite too close for comfort, Charlie." Kit scanned the glaring snow beyond the cave. "You keep a sharp eye out, now. I've got a feeling Broken Nose is about ready to move his boys in for the kill."

"That Mexican lit out on us, Kit," Bent growled, reloading his rifle.

"Reckon it looks that way."

"I swear I'll find him. I'll run his worthless hide into the ground if I have to!"

Kit saw movement and swung his rifle, but before he could fire, a bullet ricocheted off the sandstone, spraying stinging sand into his face. He flattened against the wall and said, "Let's worry about getting out of here first. Pass me one of them spare rifles."

Bent slid a rifle across to Kit. Kit checked the cap and set it nearby, where he could get a hand on it quickly if the Comanches decided to charge the cave.

"It's just that it makes me so angry. It's because of him we are in this pickle barrel in the first place. And because he's such an gaunt little fellow, he manages to squirm his way out of it while we're stuck here to pay for his sins." Bent stewed a while longer, then said more calmly, almost as if speaking to himself, "Hell, Kit, I haven't been married but a week. Ignacia has already been widowed once, I don't want to put her through that again—at least not anytime soon." He looked at Kit. "And it's your birthday. A hell of a way to spend it, isn't it?"

"I reckon we both have something to moan about if we allow it."

"Today will be your *death*-day, Carson," Wilson put in, laughing at his little joke.

Seth Wilson's needling was grinding at Kit's nerves. Over the past hours, Kit's determination to bring the man to justice—alive—had slowly dissolved. He had half decided that a simple letter to Colonel Holmes explaining that he had found his daughter's tormentor and that the scoundrel had been dealt with according to Western justice would suit Kit's purposes now. Kit was only looking for an excuse to be shed of Wilson, and right then any old provocation would work just fine. But Kit eased back on his anger. Like he had warned Charles Bent, they first had to figure a way out of their present predicament. Afterwards, he'd have time to deal with Wilson.

Their horses had not been bothered by the Comanches since he'd shot one of the Indians making an attempt at them. Well, why risk men on something you were going to eventually get your hands on anyway, Kit thought wryly. All at once the hairs at the back of his neck stiffened. Kit hadn't seen anything to cause the alarm, but somehow he knew that something was about to happen.

"What is it?" Bent asked, sensing Kit's sudden wariness.

"Thar moving."

Bent squinted across the bright snow. "Where?"

Below, a dark buffalo robe suddenly flashed against the glaring snow near the rocks that concealed their horses. Kit swung and fired. Bent snapped off a shot in another direction, at a second fleeting figure. Suddenly the bushes seemed to come alive with men dodging this way and that. Kit grabbed up the spare rifle and fired. Bent sent a bullet crashing into the bushes to his left. Belatedly Kit realized what had happened. The Comanches had lured them with decoys, deliberately drawing their fire! What Kit and Bent were shooting at weren't men at all, but the Indians' buffalo robes held out on poles.

Kit hastily started reloading his rifle, but before he could ram a ball down the barrel, the Comanches suddenly rose up from their many places of concealment and released a volley of arrows that forced Kit and Bent away from the mouth of the cave. Immediately the Indians cried out a wild yell and charged up from the canyon floor.

Kit cursed himself for his stupidity. The Comanches had caught them with their rifles empty—exactly as they had planned it! He grabbed for his pistol left-handed. But just as he pulled it free, the crack of another pistol echoed up the canyon.

The sound of it coming from the north not only drew Kit's eye, it had the same effect on the Comanches, who had not been expecting to hear gunfire from that quarter. For an instant, movement in the canyon came to a halt; time froze for a heartbeat. Then like distant thunder, a low rumbling began to grow, swelling in volume.

Kit glanced out of the cave. To his amazement, the Comanches had reversed their charge and were now scrambling toward the canyon's floor. To the north, Kit watched the horses pouring from the side canyon, turning together as a flock of birds might to some unseen guiding hand, and pounding at a full gallop down the main canyon.

Chapter Fourteen

"He did it!" Bent exclaimed, his mouth falling open in amazement at the sight of Hernando astride one of the galloping horses, expertly driving the herd not down and out of the canyon as would be expected, but straight for the Comanches' position. "The Mexican didn't run out on us after all!"

"He's trying to run them down!" Kit declared.

"And they're scattering like chickens in a road!" Bent said excitedly.

Kit was momentarily transfixed by the sight of the horses pounding closer and the rumbling sound of their hooves booming between the canyon's walls. Hernando was giving them the chance they needed to get away, and Kit knew they needed to move out now, before the Comanches regrouped.

As the horses swerved sharply and veered toward the canyon wall, the Comanches scrambled to higher ground. He and Bent had only a few moments before the horses would pass through the scattered war party. Kit couldn't count on the Comanches breaking off the attack to follow their fleeing horses.

He shoved his pistol under his belt and glanced at Bent. "Hernando's giving us some breathing room, Charlie. Let's use it!"

The two men hauled Wilson to his feet and hustled him down to their waiting horses. Hands still bound, the wounded man stumbled weakly between them along the rocky, snow-covered trail. They kept him moving in spite of his difficulty, and roughly hoisted him up onto his saddle. Kit quickly untied the animals as Bent swung up onto his own mount.

The wild herd thundered past them, making their own animals stomp and rise up, catching the stampede's enthusiasm. Kit clutched the reins of his and Wilson's horses, and those of the pack animal, in his left hand, fighting the horses' natural urge to run with the others. Bent sawed at his reins, keeping his animal in check. Through the commotion, Kit spied one of the Comanches clambering onto a rock and making a daring leap into the charging herd, landing expertly upon the back of one of the passing ponies. Twisting his fingers into the horse's flying mane, the Indian yanked the pony's head to one side and broke it free from the rest of the animals.

The horses finally swept past Kit's position, and the last that he saw of the Comanche, the Indian was lying low to the wind, flying across the snow-covered ground toward the stampeding herd . . . and Hernando.

Calming the horses, Kit swung into his saddle and turned his animal onto a trail winding down to the bottom of the canyon. They had gone but a few hundred feet, and had just emerged on the bottom of the canyon, when Diego suddenly appeared atop a rock off the left side of the trail and leveled his rifle at them.

"Go no farther, *Señores*," he ordered, steadying his sights on Kit's chest. "Drop those rifles."

"From the frying pan to the fire," Bent said, setting the butt of his rifle on the ground and letting it fall. "There. Not that it makes much difference. It's not loaded."

Kit followed Bent's example.

Wilson was leaning forward in the saddle, clutching his side, his face contorted in pain. "Diego!" he exclaimed, relief swelling in that single word.

"It is good to see that you are still breathing, *mi amigo*. You are bad hurt?"

"Bad enough. But it's going to take more than a pistol ball to kill me."

Beyond Diego, Kit caught a glimpse of the herd racing toward the end of the canyon, where the steep walls fell away to flatter, more open land. It was too distant to see if the Comanche had caught up with Hernando. Kit could only hope that the scrawny Mexican was able to outride one determined Indian. From what Kit had just witnessed of Hernando's horsemanship, he had no doubt that, barring a fall, Hernando could handle himself atop a horse better than most men.

Diego said, "Tell me, which one of these men is called Carson?"

Wilson straightened up a little, wincing at the pain. Fresh blood was on his hands when he pointed a finger. "It's that one there. He done it. I want the pleasure of lifting his scalp. This is the second time he put a bullet in me."

Diego's eyes widened with sudden understanding. "Ah, so this is the *hombre* you curse every night when you crawl into your bedroll. The one you have told me about, heh?"

"He's the one."

Diego motioned Kit toward Wilson. "Cut his hands free, *Señor*. You will do this one good deed before the devil claims his own."

Kit had learned long ago that when a man argues with a rifle, he often loses much more than just the argument. Frowning, Kit moved his horse alongside Wilson's. At the canyon's end, where it spilled out onto the plains, Kit saw a single horse veering away from the stampeding herd and heading back into the canyon.

"Where are Broken Nose and his warriors?" Kit asked, stalling.

"His warriors? Most are dead, *Señor* Carson, because of you. Broken Nose, he is very angry. But it is a very dangerous thing for the Comanches to be on foot so far from their lodges. Those left, they rushed away to catch up with the horses. But they will be back. Unfortunately for you, it will be too late. You and your *amigo* will be dead." Diego grinned. "The chief will be most grateful to me, I think. We will do much trading with him, heh, Wilson? His horses will bring many pesos in the marketplace."

"And your guns will cause many deaths among the settlers," Kit said evenly.

Diego shrugged his shoulders, his rifle drifting a bit off of Kit. "It is the price many will pay. The West, it is not an easy place to come to, no? The strong, they will make it. The weak, they will not."

"That includes women and children," Kit said.

"It is not my concern. A man is a fool to bring women and children to a land like this. They should stay in the East, where all the Indians have been conquered. This I can say, the white man will have a very hard time conquering the Comanches."

"Especially with you supplying them with rifles."

"It is business."

Charles Bent said, "I know something of business, *Señor*, and there is a place where a man must draw the line. Profit at any cost quickly turns a man's heart to stone. It shrivels his soul!"

"And who are you?"

"Charles Bent."

Diego looked surprised. "I know of you. You are very wealthy. Your trading house does much business, no? Do you not sell to the Indians too?"

"I carry on a strong trade with the Indians. Seldom does it include guns."

"*Seldom?* Ah, then it is only the amount that bothers you? It seems we are both fishing in the same pond, *Señor* Bent." Diego returned his dark gaze to Kit. "Now, cut *Señor* Wilson's hands free."

Kit's eyes had been trailing the distant rider. As he drew nearer, Kit saw that it was Hernando. The Comanche, it seemed, was not pursuing him, but had decided to remain with the horses and try to bring them to a stop. Out of long habit, Kit reached for the butcher knife under his coat with his right hand, even though the mauled hand was practically useless for grabbing and holding a knife now.

"No, *Señor* Carson." Diego's words stopped him. "The other hand, *por favor*. I have seen what you can do. Use the left hand."

Kit slipped his left hand under the coat and to his surprise his fist wrapped automatically around the pistol he'd thrust there. He'd forgotten it was there, but now a plan sprang to life. Kit paused, as if just then seeing something, then nodded his head toward the valley and said, "A rider's coming, Diego. He's not a Comanche, is he a friend of yours?"

Diego's eyebrows lifted questioningly. He cast a quick glance out across the canyon. Seeing Hernando, he looked again, harder this time.

Kit yanked the pistol from his belt.

Wilson shouted a warning. "Diego! He's got a gun!"

The Mexican's head snapped back around.

As he brought the pistol up a small voice at the back of Kit's brain was warning him that it had been the left-handed shot that had missed its mark and only wounded Seth Wilson the night before . . . and Diego was an even farther-off target now. But Kit didn't have time to think about that. He didn't have the luxury of even a half second to aim. Diego was already shouldering his rifle. For Kit, it would have to be a snap shot taken on the fly.

He thumbed the hammer and squeezed the trigger.

The pistol barked and leaped in his hand. With the sharp report of the gunshot still ringing in the cold, dry air, Kit threw himself off the right side of his horse. Freezing snow filled the collar of his heavy coat as he hit the ground. He covered his head with his arms and rolled off the trial, ducking the dancing hooves of his startled horse. He still didn't know if he had hit Diego, and when he did manage a glance, Diego was no longer on top of the rock.

Either his bullet had found its mark, or Diego had slipped away and was even now stalking him. Kit grabbed for his tomahawk, but his fingers stubbornly refused to close around it. Switching to his left hand, he awkwardly drew the short ax out.

Behind him Bent gave a warning shout.

Kit whirled around. It wasn't Diego! A Comanche had leaped from behind a scrawny juniper and was drawing back the gut-string of his bow. Kit dove for the cellar as the arrow whistled past his ear. Instantly, Kit was back on his feet, and he sprang for the Indian before he had time to nock another arrow. Out of the corner of his eye, Kit saw that Bent had swung off his horse and was desperately feeling around inside his coat for something.

The Comanche flung the bow aside and reached under his buffalo robe. Steel glinted in the lowering sunlight as his short skinning knife appeared suddenly.

"Are you the killer of dogs?" the Comanche demanded in Spanish as they circled, testing each other at first.

Kit recognized the voice. "It was me, Broken

Nose. I killed those dogs and some of your boys too."

The Comanche lunged.

Kit leaped back, slicing empty air with his tomahawk. The Comanche's fierce eyes latched onto Kit's, darkening with murderous intent. His long, black hair hung in a loose, wild fringe about his neck and shoulders as he moved with a powerful, cat-like ease. Kit would have to call upon everything he'd ever learned about Indian fighting to come out of this battle alive.

He tried to flex his fingers, to work some usefulness into them, but the hand had swollen so large it refused to function anymore.

A glance past the Comanche's shoulder showed Charles Bent over by the rock, groping around in the snow for something. . . .

The knife struck upward with a suddenness that almost caught him off guard.

Kit twisted away from the lunge and parried with a swipe of his tomahawk. But, left-handed as it was, Kit's reply was easily dodged. Sweat streaked Kit's forehead in spite of the cold as they circled each other, their frozen breath a gray veil hanging between them. Kit ached all over from the ordeal of the last day and a half, and all he wanted was rest, but not the sort of *permanent* rest this Comanche was offering him.

The Comanche made a quick jog to the left. Kit saw a brief opening and struck out. He was too slow. His tomahawk glanced off the Indian's thick buffalo robe. Instantly, the Comanche rounded on him. Kit threw up his right arm to block the knife, and at the same time scrambled back a step. His heel slammed into a rock, and before Kit could shuffle his feet to regain his balance, he was falling backwards.

The landing wrenched every one of his already tortured back muscles. His hand slammed into a rock, sending a firestorm of pain surging up his arm. Seeing his advantage, the Comanche dropped atop Kit, pinning his left arm beneath a knee and locking strong fingers around his throat. Broken Nose raised the knife for the final plunge.

Kit flung his aching right arm up to knock aside the knife. A rifle boomed and the Indian lurched forward. Kit rolled out from under him as the man fell facedown in the snow. His fingers groped a moment, then went still.

Kit looked over to the rock, where Charlie Bent stood, an eye still slanted along the barrel of Diego's rifle, gray smoke hanging in the air above its muzzle as if frozen in place. He let out a low groan and slowly sat up.

"Whal, it sure took you long enough, Charlie."

Bent lowered the rifle. "I couldn't find my pistol, Kit. Must have lost it back in the cave. Luckily I saw where this gun fell, but I couldn't hardly find the damned thing under all this snow. And when I finally did, I wasn't even certain it would fire."

Kit suddenly remembered the Mexican. "Diego?" His view shot to the tall rock behind Bent.

"You got him, Kit. A nice bit of shooting. Maybe you won't need all that target practice you were talking about after all."

Kit managed a grin, and a wave of relief spread through him as he sat in the snow, feeling all done in. Bent started over to give him a hand up.

Still astride his horse, Wilson leaned forward.

"Is this the gun you lost, Bent?" His bound hands came up, and in them was Charles Bent's pistol. Wilson gave a mocking look of surprise. "Well, well, looks like I'm the only one here left holding a loaded gun. What do you think about that? You ought to be more careful with it, Mr. Merchantman." He laughed briefly before his face hardened. "Step away from Carson. It might be a little cumbersome with my hands tied, but I can still shoot just fine." He gave a small wave of the pistol.

Bent stopped, his eyes swinging from side to side, seemingly unable to decide if he should be watching Kit or Wilson.

Kit nodded for Bent to retreat.

The businessman took a step backward.

"All right, Carson, now we settle up, you and me."

"I seem to recollect we done this once before. You had the pistol then too," Kit said.

"Only difference is, this time I don't intend to miss."

Kit allowed a grin, even though mirth was the furthest thing from his mind. "Now that's a revelation to me, Wilson. I didn't think you intended to miss the first time."

Wilson's scowl cut deep into his face, and his knuckles whitened as his fist tightened about the pistol.

Kit's whole attention was on Wilson, and he was only half-aware of a sound growing louder off to one side. Wilson had only one shot, but at this close range, Kit couldn't hope that it would go wide, not like it had two years earlier.

Wilson said, "You tried this the last time, Carson. You figuring to talk my ear off again, or is this your sorry effort to keep on breathing a few seconds longer? Because if it is, it ain't gonna work this time." The pistol was already cocked. Wilson lifted his hands and narrowed an eye behind the sight.

The sound that Kit had been hearing swelled suddenly. The pounding of hoofbeats caught Wilson's ear too. Surprised, he turned his head.

A blur swept past Kit. A horse thundered by, and as it did, Hernando sprang from its back and rocketed into Wilson. The two collided with a smack that propelled Wilson off his horse and both men to the ground. As they landed together, Kit heard the report of the pistol going off, muffled by their bodies.

Kit scrambled to his feet. Bent was already moving. Hernando and Wilson were lying in a heap off to the side of the trail, and neither one of them was moving.

Chapter Fifteen

Kit grabbed Wilson by the arm and dragged him off of Hernando. Wilson offered no resistance; there was no fight in him. Blood covered both men.

"Hernando?" Bent said, kneeling beside the skinny man and taking him by his shoulders, shaking gently. When he got no response, Bent opened the Mexican's coat and began searching for a bullet wound.

Kit turned back to Wilson and pressed a finger aside his neck. He frowned and said to Bent, "This one is dead."

"The pistol?" Bent said, glancing at the weapon lying between the two men. It didn't take long for them to find the hole beneath Wilson's beard where the bullet had entered the man's chin. Kit could not find an exit wound and had to conclude that the bullet had come to rest in Wilson's brain, killing him instantly.

A soft moan brought them back to the Mexican. Hernando's eyes fluttered open and he looked around, dazed. He blinked a couple of times, as if trying to clear his vision. "*Señor* Bent . . . *Señor* Carson?" he mumbled groggily, his eye finding the trapper leaning over him. Hernando's hand reached feebly for the back of his head. It was then that Kit spied the blood matting Hernando's thick black hair, and the rock beneath him where he had fallen.

"You got yourself a pretty bad bump thar, Hernando."

"But you are not hurt?" Hernando asked.

"No, I'm not. Thanks to you. That was a mighty brave thing you done, Hernando," Kit said.

"A damned crazy stunt, if you ask me," Bent allowed.

Hernando gave a small grin.

Kit said, "You were free. Why did you come back?"

"I had to come back, *Señor* Carson. You see, I knew that Wilson had taken the *pistola*. I should have told you about it at once, but I was afraid of what he might do. At first I thought to run away, but when I had the chance to do so, something inside me would not allow it." He gave a wry grin, as if embarrassed by this apparent weakness. "I am a thief, no?"

Kit nodded his head.

"But I am not a murderer, and I could not be a party to murder."

"I reckon you've got a mite more character than I allowed, Hernando."

The Mexican's grin widened.

Charles Bent looked out across the canyon's floor and said nervously, "We need to get moving, Kit, before those Comanches gather in their ponies and come back looking for us."

Kit said to Hernando, "Think you can ride?"

"I will try." When they helped him to his feet, Hernando swayed and staggered, stabbing back a leg to stop the fall. Kit and Bent helped him onto his horse. Before leaving, they reloaded their weapons, then gathered up the packhorse with the two crates of rifles. Neither Bent nor Kit wanted to leave them behind for the Comanches to take, and Bent couldn't stand to see valuable trade items like rifles being lost.

Kit only shook his head in wonderment. After all they had been through, Bent was still thinking like a businessman. It was no wonder the man was wealthy . . . and Kit was not. Swinging up onto their mounts, Kit cast one final look back at Seth Wilson. Then the three men started for Taos—and home. He had always known there would come a day of reckoning, and now that it was here, he felt no real satisfaction.

Colonel Holmes would have to be notified about Wilson's demise—he would want to know about it. Kit knew he could have his friend, Gray Feather, put his words onto paper for him, a skill Kit had never learned. That, perhaps, would hold some satisfaction.

So many had died these two days. Kit tried not to think about that, but even if he could bury the thought for the present, it would only lie dormant in his memory for just so long before resurfacing.

The sight of death is a haunting specter, one a man never quite forgets. . . .

The three men reached Taos well after nightfall, and Kit was relieved to see the lights of the village twinkling below. His hand ached miserably, and Charles Bent had promised that his new bride, Ignacia, had soaking salts and a poultice that would draw out the infection and the pain, and put his hand "right as rain" in just a few days.

They reined to a stop atop a low hill and watched a procession down a narrow street. Worshipers on their way to church for Christmas Eve services carried torches that flickered upon the brown adobe walls of the homes on either side of the street. Along the street burned small bonfires, *luminarias*, and in spite of the bitter cold, a good many people were out and about. There was a friendly, festive feeling in the air.

Outside the church the worshipers extinguished their torches and deposited them in an adobe holder that looked a little like the top of a well. At the church door they were greeted by the priest before going inside.

The sky was cloudless and startlingly clear. Brittle-cold air made the starlight leap out with a stark clarity that was somehow missing on warm summer evenings.

They peered across the town to Don Francisco's adobe, where tendrils of smoke rose from all four chimneys. Kit glanced at Bent and caught his eye.

"What's that look for, Kit?"

Hernando's horse was between them and the Mexican was huddled deep in his sheepskin coat. A bandage peeked out from beneath his hat. Hernando hadn't said but a handful of words since leaving the canyon behind.

"You have Don Francisco's gold, you said?"

Bent patted his pocket. "Right here."

Kit frowned. "Reckon he'll be right pleased just to have it back, don't you think?"

"I suppose. Wouldn't you?"

Kit rocked back in his saddle and blew a cloud of steam into his fist. "You know, if it wasn't for Hernando, we'd both still be back in that cave. Probably dead by now."

"If it wasn't for Hernando, we wouldn't have been in that cave in the first place," Bent returned brusquely.

Kit nodded his head. "That's true, but the fact is, when Hernando had the chance to cut loose and head for the high lonesome to save his own hide, he didn't. He came back, and if he hadn't, my scalp would be decorating Seth Wilson's rifle right now—and yours would be on its way to Broken Nose's lodge pole."

"Well . . ." Bent drew the word out thoughtfully, mulling it over some. "What exactly is it you're getting at, Kit?"

"Getting at? Why, Charlie, what a suspicious nature you have. I'm not getting at anything at all . . . except that if Hernando were to get it in his head all of a sudden to light a shuck for La Madera and take up with that filly with the eyes like rock coal and a touch softer than an angel's whisper, whal, right now I'd not be much inclined to go after him and haul him back."

Bent laughed. "You sure went the long way 'round the barn to say we ought to let the thief go."

Kit grinned. "Reckon I did at that."

Hernando's head poked out from the tall collar of his coat, and curiosity glinted in his eyes as they shifted between the two men.

Bent thought it over a moment, then said, "I wouldn't want it to ever get out that we just let him go."

Kit agreed. "Considering the cold, and my aching hand, and the plain fact that I haven't had any sleep in two days, and you napped only a few minutes back in that cave, It wouldn't take a whole lot of effort for a sly fellow like Hernando to sneak away from us, don't you think?"

"I can see how it might happen," Bent allowed.

"*Señores*, I know what you are doing, and I appreciate it, but no. I will not run away. I have done a crime against my *patrón*, and I will take my punishment."

Hernando's announcement almost knocked Kit from his saddle. "What about Juanita?"

Hernando frowned. "She is the love of my life. The apple of my eye," he said sadly. "But I have had much time to think it over. I fear the feeling is not the same for her."

"Really?" Bent said.

"*Sí, Señor* Bent. For if she felt for me what I feel for her, then money would not matter. Even if her father disapproved, she would go with me. But it is not so. I think this is something I must give more consideration to, no? A few years in the alcalde's prison will give me much time to think. What I have done was wrong. It has cost the lives of many men, and you two almost died because of me. I am ready to face Don Francisco Jaramillo now."

Kit and Bent were speechless. Kit finally broke the silence. "This child's ears don't hardly believe what they're hearing right now." He looked at Bent. "Reckon a good word from Don Francisco's new son-in-law might make him go a little easier on Hernando?"

"I can try. Can't promise anything, though."

"It is all right," Hernando said. "I will take my punishment. It is only right. Afterwards, I can make a new start, and if it is meant to be, then Juanita will be waiting for me. If not . . ." he shrugged his shoulders, resigned to his fate, "is it not better the alcalde's prison for a few years than the prison of an unhappy marriage for life?"

"Such pearls of wisdom, Hernando. I am impressed," Bent said.

Kit could only shake his head in amazement as they got their horses moving again. The three of them rode down through the middle of Taos, and as they passed by the church with the worshipers arriving for the Christmas Eve service, Hernando averted his eyes and lowered his head. Quickly, secretly, he crossed himself . . . and then they had passed the church and the Mexican lifted his gaze toward the large adobe house where they were headed.

They had recovered Don Francisco Jaramillo's gold, were bringing the thief back to justice, and Kit had settled up an old account with Seth Wilson. So why did he feel so hollow inside?

Then a thought brought a small grin to his face. If he had come away with anything from this adventure, he had learned one thing. A polecat really can change the color of his stripes—that is, if the polecat was an honorable little fellow named Hernando.

171

DAVY CROCKETT

HOMECOMING

DAVID THOMPSON

Davy Crockett lives for adventure. With a faithful friend at his side and a trusty long rifle in his hand, the fearless frontiersman sets out for the Great Lakes territories. But the region surrounding the majestic inland seas is full of Indians both peaceful and bloodthirsty. And when the brave pioneer saves a Chippewa maiden from warriors of a rival tribe, his travels become a deadly struggle to save his scalp. If Crockett can't defeat his fierce foes, the only remains he'll leave will be his legend and his coonskin cap.

___4112-X $3.99 US/$4.99 CAN

Dorchester Publishing Co., Inc.
P.O. Box 6640
Wayne, PA 19087-8640

Please add $1.75 for shipping and handling for the first book and $.50 for each book thereafter. NY, NYC, and PA residents, please add appropriate sales tax. No cash, stamps, or C.O.D.s. All orders shipped within 6 weeks via postal service book rate. Canadian orders require $2.00 extra postage and must be paid in U.S. dollars through a U.S. banking facility.

Name_____
Address_____
City_____State_____Zip_____
I have enclosed $_____ in payment for the checked book(s).
Payment <u>must</u> accompany all orders. ❏ Please send a free catalog.